RUNNING DEAD

RUNNING DEAD

ROSS CROTHERS

Ginger Marks Cover design and Layout
DocUmeantDesigns, www.DocUmeantDesigns.com

Jason and Marina Anderson Formatting and Publishing Services
Polgarus Studio, www.polgarusstudio.com

Philip S Marks Editor

Printed in Australia
ISBN: 978-0-6481771-1-1 (paperback)

DEDICATION

For Netts

CHAPTER ONE

Terry Walker was beginning to feel like a million quid. In fact, maybe like forty or fifty million. It was a long time since he had ridden in a car like this, but he was getting used to it again, fast. London is a beautiful city; but a damn sight more beautiful when wrapped in the fluted leather and walnut veneer of this particular vehicle.

At sixty-two, he found work boring and uninspiring, particularly at the shipping brokerage on Oxford Street where he now found himself employed. Business had once been so good, exciting even, but that seemed like a lifetime ago. Now there was a chance, maybe only slim, but a chance nevertheless, that he could regain all he had lost.

"Nice car Andrew," he said, casting his glance around the interior, as they glided quietly along Marylebone Road, "and thanks for picking me up. What make is it again?"

"Bentley Continental GT... coupe," replied Andrew Lau, maneuvering his pride and joy, his Chinese accent still very noticeable over otherwise perfectly clipped English. "Don't you just love the smell of it?" They swung right in to Gloucester Place, left into Dorset Square, then down three blocks before turning left into Harewood Avenue. One block down then left again, and eased into the hotel driveway.

What a wonderful building thought Walker, squinting hard as he stared up at the facade. But then again, London was all wonderful buildings. "Who is it again we are meeting?"

"No name," replied Lau, "only a room number... 460. But this time I think we will be okay. This time, after ten years, I think we'll get the money."

"I hope you're right... I could do with it," said Walker in a barely audible whisper.

Two regally clad doormen opened the car doors simultaneously. "Welcome to The Landmark, any luggage gentlemen?"

"No, we'll only be about an hour, please look after the car for me," said Lau, unobtrusively sliding a twenty into the doorman's palm.

They entered the elegant foyer and Lau strode purposefully towards the lift with Walker following hurriedly behind. Shit he dresses well thought Walker... when we get this money I'm going to visit his tailor. *Another* trip to Hong Kong I guess. The thought of *that* made him feel good again, if only for an instant.

The lift rose swiftly and silently up to level four. Walker intently watched the floor numbers light up, as if to make doubly sure they got it right. The two men marched in time along the plush carpeted hallway, and Lau gave three sharp raps on the door of 460.

"Come in," replied a female voice from inside.

Andrew Lau pushed open the door and stepped into the suite, with Walker following, now tentatively, behind. A grey-haired male figure was silhouetted against the huge window, his back to the men, but there was no sign of any female.

Two armchairs were arranged side-by-side, also facing the window.

"Please sit!" directed the male voice. Each gently sank into an armchair and said nothing. "I believe you are seeking *more* money," continued the silhouette without turning around.

"That is correct," replied Lau, "and yesterday you recall we spoke to . . ."

"It is not important who you spoke to," interrupted the shadow, "it is just a pity you cannot leave things alone. You push *too hard*!"

Lau glanced at Walker and shrugged his shoulders, thrown by the outburst.

"Now, I understand you know my assistant?" asked the shadow.

"Gentlemen," purred a female voice behind the two men. Andrew Lau turned in his chair but before he had reached halfway round a muffled shot rang out. The side of Lau's head exploded sending a spray of blood onto the sheer curtains.

Terry Walker snapped around toward the gunshot, his face ashen. For a brief, stunned moment he stared at the female figure before him.

"What the f . . ." he stammered, but before he could finish, a second shot took him straight through the right temple.

The male figure finally turned from the window and looked over the two bodies crumpled in blood before him. He half-looked up at the woman standing there. The corners of his mouth flickered; the faintest hint of a smile.

"Good job," he said, "now I think it's best we leave."

CHAPTER TWO

Detective Chief Inspector McClure was tired. All day in meetings of the detective management unit, discussing tactics, reporting on progress, facts, figures, and mind numbing banality. After thirty years with Scotland Yard he still liked the *real* police work. The stuff on the street... that's what he lived for. These end on end-on-end meetings, where nothing was ever resolved, made him feel every bit his fifty-two years.

Now he had a call to go to The Landmark Hotel. Despite the late afternoon traffic, particularly around the Palace, the trip was swift. McClure's driver pulled into the hotel forecourt and eased the black Ford to a stop. Met vehicles were everywhere, lights swirling, headlights ablaze, crime scene tape sealing the entrance from the public. "This is more like it," thought McClure ... "meaty stuff, *proper* cop work."

McClure flashed his badge at the young constable standing in the hotel doorway. "Afternoon Chief Inspector ... it's level four you want." McClure nodded, said nothing and strode through the hotel lobby.

With driver in tow, McClure arrived at Room 460 to be greeted by Sergeant Shepherd, a beefy, grey-haired sixty-four year old, who'd overseen more crime scenes than he cared to remember. The forensics in their white suits were trawling the floor, the furniture and the curtains, minutely extracting remnants deposited by a myriad of guests. It occurred to the sergeant as he watched on quietly, people have no idea what they *really* leave behind.

"What have we got, Sergeant?" asked McClure. He and Shepherd had been mates in the force for a long time, but at moments like this, formality was the order of the day.

"Bloody hell of a mess sir ... two dead males ... two single gunshots it looks like," Shepherd replied dryly.

"Jesus!" muttered McClure, as he gingerly stepped over the body of Andrew Lau. "Any names?"

"Licences say Andrew Lau and Terence Walker," the sergeant replied. McClure bent over the buckled, lifeless bodies and peered at each face. Lau's in particular was missing a bit, but those faces—he knew them alright! What had they done to *cause this*?

"Can I sit here?" McClure asked one of the forensics. "Yes sir, we're done there," replied the officer. McClure slumped on the hotel bed, his mind processing the mess before him.

"It's been ten years Shep," continued McClure, talking to the sergeant but addressing no one in particular, "and these two were part of one of the biggest fraud cases I've ever investigated. But they were never partners . . . they only ever came together in a courtroom. Why would they be together now after all these years . . . and *dead*?"

There was a long period of silence. McClure's mind was obviously somewhere else on the planet. Sergeant Shepherd busied himself helping the forensics . . . best not to look too bored, keep active until the boss comes up with something.

"Sergeant," McClure said again, still addressing no one in particular, "I don't think I can do this on my own—but there is one person who can help us get to the bottom of it . . . let's get him here."

CHAPTER THREE

I peered out the porthole of Qantas Flight One as it taxied slowly up to the Heathrow terminal. Light misty rain sent small rivulets down the window. Why was it always damp here, I wondered? Ten years since my last visit, and it was damp then. So it must *always* be damp.

I thought of Sydney. Little more than twenty-four hours ago I had woken in my apartment in Elizabeth Bay, looking out over Sydney Harbour to a clear, warm morning. Everything was blue and sparkling! I usually rise about six, stroll three doors to the deli for the daily paper, then with coffee in hand sit on my terrace above the harbour, and watch as Sydney comes to life. And so it was yesterday.

I thought of Sally. She is beautiful, but after six months together she seems to be a little distant. Maybe it was her work; big law firms seem to suck the life out of their people. Maybe a short break would do us both good.

Then Jim McClure rang. I hadn't heard from him for years and his call was a bolt from the blue. We had worked really well together solving the Connolly fraud case ten years earlier. After all this time a call from Jim could only mean one thing . . . *a complicated issue!*

He wouldn't give details . . . just that it involved people from the Connolly trial and he needed my help. *His* office had cleared it with *my* office, and all the usual crap. So I boarded the first available flight. At least it left at a respectable hour in the afternoon . . . and these days as a senior officer of the Australian Federal Police I got to travel in business. Just as well too! At six feet five and two hundred and seventy-five pounds, twenty-four hours back in cattle class would be like two years in solitary.

The process through Heathrow Customs was quick. Always is for Federal coppers. And my bags were hand-delivered to me the moment Customs was finished. Maybe that was another plus for international travel I thought . . . no, let's not get carried away.

As I stepped through the automatic doors there was Jim McClure to greet me. He hadn't changed much... maybe a bit greyer but otherwise the same young-looking face. English weather I guess... not like that hard Australian sun. I thought of Sydney again. And he kept himself fit.

"Detective Commander Ashley Todd," exclaimed McClure, "it is good to see you again. Thank you for coming so quickly. And my goodness you haven't shrunk at all," he said grinning.

"You haven't changed either," I said, "except maybe around the temples. Grecian 2000 I believe, is very effective."

"Now, now," he said good-naturedly, "you'll have plenty of time later to become nasty and vindictive."

"So, why am I here and what's with all the cloak and dagger?"

"Let's get to the car," replied McClure, "and I'll tell everything I know, so far."

CHAPTER FOUR

We sat in the back of DCI McClure's black Met limo, slipped on to the M4 heading for the city, and he began to fill me in.

"Where to begin?" he asked. "You remember at the Connolly trial two of the most active complainants were a New Zealander ... a Maori looking fellow ... called Terry Walker."

"I do," I replied cutting in, "he had quite a successful shipping business operating around the Pacific Islands, but after the trial I heard no more of him."

"Not surprising," said McClure, "I think the cost of trying to do business with Connolly, and the cost of the trial, broke him. He shut the business down after twelve months, then moved here to London. The last three or four years he's been working in town for a shipping broker ... but from our investigation has been only just getting by."

"And the other bloke?" I asked. "Which one ... we had seven or eight people who were after Connolly for the money they wasted on him?"

"Andrew Lau," replied McClure, "remember him? Chinese chap from Hong Kong, educated here in London, ran a very successful exporting business from China, mostly into Australia."

"Yeah, yeah," I said, recalling the immaculately dressed Lau. "Christ, didn't Connolly take some money from those two ... from everyone really ... but Walker and Lau must have spent £200,000 or £300,000 each on him, chasing loans of £40 or £50 million."

"And not one penny of it arrived," continued McClure in disgust, "millions wasted on a two-bob conman."

"But his story was so good wasn't it? You remember ... magnificent estate in Kent, villa in Tuscany, meetings to attend with his bankers on Wall Street, even trips to the Caribbean ... all in the line of duty, of course."

"Absolutely," said McClure, "and he had to be jetted around the world, first-class, paid for by the likes of Walker and Lau, to attend meetings with them ... and the loan money was always just about to arrive."

"As you said, not one cent materialised ... and then the judge found nothing existed ... there was no estate ... no villa ... the bank meetings never happened. None of them existed and the money certainly didn't exist. Except in Connolly's head. No wonder nothing turned up! So, what are Walker and Lau up to?"

"Well, Walker has been working here for some years as I mentioned. And about a week ago Lau flew in from Australia. So far as we know he came here to do business ... but we aren't sure what sort of business."

"Okay, that I get, but other than their mutual interest in Connolly I don't imagine they would have much in common. So what's the link between them now?"

"They're dead," said McClure straight-faced, "single shot through the head ... both of them ... together ... in the same hotel room."

Together! I was dumbfounded. But I was now beginning to understand why McClure wanted me here so fast.

CHAPTER FIVE

We travelled the rest of the trip to the Metropolitan Police headquarters in Victoria in comparative silence. I was trying to get all the old pieces together in my mind ... ten years is a long time and so many cases since ... it took a while to recall the events clearly.

McClure's office was expansive ... fifth floor on the corner, but with a fairly ordinary outlook across Dacre Street at the neighbouring buildings. Still he had a huge, handsome, timber desk and leather chair for himself, and a long, studded, leather ottoman filled one wall. At least the trappings of seniority allowed something other than regulation, Yard-grey laminate.

"So," I said finally, "let me recap. Firstly Walker ... he had his shipping business and from memory wanted to borrow about £20 million to expand his fleet... and he paid about £200,000 to Connolly who'd promised him the money."

"Correct," said McClure, "and with a no-show on the dough he'd lost everything, marriage included, though I believe he's found a new live-in lover here. Had to take a lowly job to survive. Therefore I think we can assume the money was required to more than just upgrade the fleet... prop up the whole show is my guess."

"No wonder he was bitter when it all folded. These things always cause a double whammy. Even though the money never existed, in his mind it *was his*... so he effectively lost the money as well as the business."

"Yes," said McClure wistfully, staring at the ceiling, "that's certainly true isn't it?"

"And Andrew Lau... he wanted to get into property development. I seem to recall Connolly had promised him £40 million, and he'd shelled out the best part of four hundred big ones to aid the Connolly lifestyle. At least his business was solid... he might not *like* losing the money, but he could afford it."

"Looks like he hardly missed a beat," said McClure, "he's expanded his operation into

Europe and the UK, and it appears he owns an expensive apartment in one of those new developments at the Canary Wharf. That alone would be worth a few million."

McClure's PA, Cindy, knocked and entered offering coffee, which I accepted gratefully. Attractive girl I thought, but then that made me think of Sydney ... and Sally. The long flight was beginning to catch up with me, and I needed something to keep me awake ... espresso and Cindy might do the trick ... and I took a sip.

The weak, milky taste hit the back of my tongue, and I winced. God, I thought, the Metropolitan Police could do with a crash-course in caffeine presentation. Still, it snapped me into the present.

"And Connolly," I asked sarcastically, "I assume he served his time and has rejoined society as a productive, paid-up member?"

"Heard nothing of him," McClure dead-panned, "but I've got the team checking on his whereabouts ... see if we can find any movement on him in the last couple of years. At his court case he seemed to have spent all the money, and he supposedly owned nothing, so

I have no idea where he'd go when he was released. Might be dead for all we know."

"I reckon he could still have friends from his money lending days. Despite what the judge said, I always thought it strange that someone could travel the world offering megabucks, and have absolutely *no* connection to any source of money. After all, his tentacles spread fairly wide ... there were plenty more borrowers than Walker and Lau, all with shitloads of money ... it's just that they were the ones who decided to chase him."

"True, but what other background did we have on him?" asked McClure.

"Well, twenty years ago Connolly was a lawyer here in London."

"That's right, I remember," said McClure, "Barkstone Associates I think it was. Law firm which specialised in investment banking."

"Yep, and they gave him some fairly influential US-based clients to look after. After a few years he left them and moved to New York. Right in amongst the Wall Street vultures. And a couple of years after that, he surfaced offering these loans. So who knows what contacts he may really have from those days?"

"And that associate of his in Australia . . . the one who introduced him to Walker and Lau and others," asked McClure, "what was his name?"

"Sands," I replied, "Roger Sands. Finance broker on the Gold Coast. He was supposedly part of some obscure cult which we never really got a handle on . . . but I don't think he'll be of much help. Alcoholic you know . . . case got the better of him. Died a couple of years ago, I believe."

There was a knock at McClure's door and the burly frame of Sergeant Shepherd appeared, filling most of it. "What have you got for me Shep?" asked McClure.

"You wanted us to see if we could find Connolly," replied the sergeant, "well we think we've found him. Same name, and the local police gave us a brief description which sounds about right."

"And where *exactly* might he be?" asked McClure with a wry smile.

"France," said the sergeant, straight-faced, "Toulon, France."

McClure and I looked at each other incredulously.

"How about that?" I exclaimed. "*The bastard's on the Riviera.*"

Chapter Six

I was weary. Twenty-three hours of flying from Sydney, then half a dozen more meeting with McClure was taking its toll. Cindy, from The Yard, had booked me into what she called a 'comfortable place' in Mayfair—Browns. "As a thank you for coming at such short notice," McClure had said, and then with a quick wink at Cindy, "I think you'll like it more than the usual."

I took my leave from the meeting with McClure, and declined his invitation for dinner. Some quiet time on my own is what I needed. And I wanted to talk to Sally... to hear her voice again. If I rang shortly it would be the right time back in Sydney... early morning... before she left for work.

McClure's driver appeared and I followed him to the lifts and down to the basement car park. I slipped into the back seat and we joined the London afternoon traffic for the short trip around St James Park to the hotel. McClure was right... it *was* much nicer than the usual 'Metropolitan Police Force approved hotels for visiting guests'. The Best Western in Kensington, where they had put me up ten years earlier, was nice enough, but *this* was living.

I settled into my room and called Sally as soon as I could. No answer. That was strange... but maybe she'd gone to work.

I ordered room service which arrived promptly. Fillet mignon and a fine French burgundy seemed about right. I hoped it would be within McClure's budget. Then I got to thinking about the case again.

My Masters in Forensic Psychology was a fancy degree, and had rocketed me up the seniority ranks, but I always found the basics were the best place to begin. So let's start with motive, I thought. Walker and Lau had both spent a huge amount of money on Connolly. Connolly had done his time, and as far as we knew, was broke. But why pursue him?

Then again, we didn't even know they actually were pursuing him. What if he wasn't broke and they decided he should pay? That might give him a motive to get rid of them. But if that was true, how would *they* know he now had money?

All we had were a dozen questions and I could keep them coming all night. I decided to get some sleep and start again with McClure in the morning. I settled into the luxurious king-size bed... there seemed to be a lot of wasted space in here... and slowly drifted off.

The phone bleeped. It bleeped again and I sat up, confused. Where was I? What time was it? Whose bed is this? It all flooded back quickly, and I picked up the phone.

It was McClure. "You awake, Ash?"

I blinked and turned on the light. "You're kidding! Of course not. Leave me alone."

"Get ready for an early start tomorrow... we've got another one. You recall we discussed Walker was shacked up with a woman here in London... had been for a couple of years?"

"Of course."

"Well she's just been found... in the Thames... and she's not swimming. Gunshot to the head. Do we see a pattern here? Get some sleep and let's say we meet at my office at eight?"

Now I was wide awake! How could I get any sleep after this?

CHAPTER SEVEN

Paul Connolly gunned the black Mercedes SL 63 up the hill out of Toulon. The EasyJet flight from Gatwick in to Toulon Hyeres had been seamless enough, but any trips back to the UK made him feel nervous. This one especially so.

He let the car settle in about 135, just above the limit . . . no point attracting unnecessary police attention . . . and cruised on up the A50 until he reached the Route de Bandol exit. He slipped the car off the motorway on to D559 and the Mediterranean hove into view . . . that magnificent expanse of coastline with steep, green hills falling sharply down through storybook towns of pastel coloured buildings. Once he saw the water . . . the jagged edge of land curving from bay to bay . . . he always felt safe, and his whole body softened noticeably. Now it was time for some top-down motoring, and he pressed the dash button.

He rolled on through Sanary-Sur-Mer village and spotted a couple of working girls exiting a popular restaurant, their tiny, tight skirts and long boots giving them away instantly. One of them he knew from two weeks ago. He lightly touched the horn and waved. She gave him the finger. He laughed. "Silly damn bitch," he thought.

Connolly wound his way along the villa-lined streets overlooking the bay, and five minutes later swung into Chemin de la Gardiole and the driveway of his villa. The automatic garage doors lifted quietly, and the black Mercedes disappeared inside. He was home.

It was only three o'clock but what the heck. It was a magical, twenty-seven degree afternoon . . . a gin and tonic was called for. He mixed himself one and settled on the terrace overlooking the pool, across the tip of Embiez Island and the blue, blue Mediterranean. Now to review the events of the last twenty four hours . . . just to make sure nothing was out of place. He took a long sip of the G and T.

Early evening flight to London on passport as French Polynesian Jean Gasteau ... cab around the City and dropped off for a meeting with Alvarez at a cafe in Limehouse ... quick train ride from Limehouse to Poplar and collected the Glock 17 and cash from the pick-up on High Street ... another two-stop ride to East India, and a short five block walk to meet Juanita down by the park on the Thames, off Jamestown Way ... all good so far.

Connolly took another long draw on his gin concoction. It's a pity she had argued about the money though. How was he to know how much was really there? He just collected the moolah along with the gun, and handed it over, as directed. Too bad ... he slipped the gun from his jacket, and a quick shot up through her jaw sorted that—wonderful invention, the silencer.

He dragged the dead-weight body of Juanita to the edge and let her slide away into the fast developing black of the evening, then wrapped the pistol in the cloth provided and replaced it inside his jacket. A moonlit stroll, no ... more a brisk walk really ... to the drop-off on Blackwall Way to ditch the cash and weapon ... keeping £5,000 for services rendered as agreed . . . back past the trains to check-in at the Travelodge, this time as Arthur Kennedy . . . again all good.

A cab to the city this morning for some window shopping . . . another cab ride back to the airport and the return flight on Belize passport as David Holding. Yes, thought Connolly smiling inwardly, everything had gone smoothly. Mission accomplished!

Shooting people was not on his CV, but the lessons from Wandsworth were coming in handy. Don't think too much, and talk even less. Besides, no-one refused an offer of work from Alvarez. To do so might abruptly terminate his own existence . . . and that made him shudder. Yes, it really was this easy, and if he thought about it, exciting too.

Still, he felt uneasy . . . had anyone *heard* Juanita Sanchez screaming profanities at him?

CHAPTER EIGHT

I arrived at McClure's office at eight as requested.

Also present were Sergeant Shepherd, who looked as though *he* had been up all night swimming in the Thames, McClure's next in line Detective Inspector Don Carty, and Sergeant Bill Moss, a young up-and-comer and a star performer in the forensic team. Oh, and Cindy, who was there to take notes should we need her. I thought she looked *easy to need.*

To get all those gathered up to speed, McClure went over the old ground we had covered the day before on Walker and Lau, and their earlier dealings with Connolly. The others sat slightly open-mouthed as they heard the vast sums involved. I grinned at Cindy. "And what would you do with all that money?" I asked. She half-smiled, put her head down and kept appearing to take notes.

"So, Sergeant Moss, can you fill us in on your discoveries to date at The Landmark Hotel?" asked McClure.

"As with all hotel rooms sir, it's a bit of a dog's breakfast. Cause of death was obvious with both victims being shot once. Bullets were Winchester... in Lau's case it passed right through him, while Walker still had it lodged in his head. The markings indicate the weapon was a Glock 17, just like ours here at the Met," replied Moss.

"Okay, anything else?"

"All our blood samples related to the two victims only. We recovered numerous hairs— I tell you it never ceases to amaze me what comes off, and out of, bodies ..."

"Thank you Sergeant, but please keep to the topic," said McClure testily.

"Sorry sir. As I was saying, numerous hairs some of which relate to the victims, and a number of others of no known origin. We got quite a lot of fingerprints and ran them over our database, but nothing has come up. One thing though, the bed had recently been *used*."

"Really!" I exclaimed, "how interesting."

"Yes," continued Moss, "and whoever was in there had been having sex. We recovered pubic hair and semen, but no DNA match with the victims."

"Maybe it was party time to celebrate the arrival of our hapless pair," I said. "And what about the room, who booked that?"

Shepherd took over. "Room was booked the day before by a woman caller for a Mr and Mrs Kater. We assume that to be a false identity. The hotel receptionist recalls a male and female arriving and registering under that name. Hotel records indicate they registered about one hour prior to the victims arriving. Policy is to request identification and they have on record a credit card and a driver's licence in the name of Raelene Kater of Kennington. We've checked the licence and it appears to be false. The room charge on the credit card was approved, and we're following up with the bank," the sergeant reported matter-of-factly.

"So what about this latest body, the woman you found last night?" I asked.

"Name's Juanita Sanchez," chimed in DI Carty, "been living with Terry Walker for about three years. Shared a flat over at Charton. Looks like she came here about ten years ago. Not much is known about her—we're tracing previous addresses—but no employment records yet. She was found floating amongst some barges at Leamouth."

"We'll have the autopsy and forensics shortly," said Moss, "she's been shot, we know that, but we need to see if there is anything else. No weapon yet, but the bullet was still in her and we've got divers scouring the river."

"And my team is doorknocking the area," added Shepherd.

"Anything else?" asked McClure. All present shook their heads. "Then I think it's time someone paid a visit to Mr Connolly—if we can find him. Ash—you feel like taking a trip to the south of France?"

South of France? Sunshine, warm weather, blue water, beautiful people... no bloody rain? You bet! Maybe Cindy would like to come along and assist? I was about to accept his kind offer when the phone rang. The flashing red light on the fourth line indicated it was forensics. McClure put on the speakerphone. "What have you got?"

"Detective Chief Inspector," the forensic voice intoned, "we have some results on the woman Juanita Sanchez. We still have no weapon, but have recovered the bullet—a 9 mm Winchester—and the markings indicate it was fired by the same weapon used to kill Walker and Lau."

Eyebrows rose round the room.

"There was no other cause. She was dead when she hit the water. The body was found at about noon yesterday—we estimate it had been in the water about fifteen to eighteen hours—therefore time of death was between six and nine p.m. the evening prior."

Well at least that was settled. Three bodies; all felled by the same weapon. And each of them related in a different way. Six degrees of separation, I thought. It wasn't much to go on, but at least it would give me some conversation starter with Connolly. *If* I could get him to talk.

"One more thing sir," continued the forensic voice, "we've done some testing of hair samples recovered from The Landmark, and we have a definite match."

"Good work," said McClure, "*who* have you got?"

"Well sir, we have pubic hair recovered from sexual activity in the Room 460 bed, and we have an exact match *for Juanita Sanchez.*"

CHAPTER NINE

McClure called 'time' on the meeting, and instructed the three officers to continue with their investigations. The last piece of evidence opened up a whole new set of questions.

Who had Sanchez had sex with in Room 460? Was it with the male who accompanied her to the hotel? If so, who was he, and what was his relationship with her? And what was his relationship with Walker and Lau? If not, *who else* was there?

McClure and I agreed . . . Connolly had to be our starting point. We really had nowhere else to begin—no leads at all. And we had nothing official on him—in fact we were assuming it *was* him in Toulon—so I would have to work up a contact plan. It was bloody flimsy, but we had no other choice. As I headed for the lifts and my hotel, Cindy was at her desk busily typing at her computer.

"I'm off to the South of France for a couple of days," I advised helpfully, "the Cote d'Azur in fact. I may need someone to run interference for me, and take notes. I've cleared it with your boss if you're interested? Strictly work of course. We will be busy."

"When are you leaving?" she asked.

"As soon as I collect my things—and you book my ticket."

"Let me check. I'll call you."

I took a cab back to my hotel and packed. I decided to leave my room booking in place—after all I had no idea how long this would take. And it would be a pity to move from Browns. McClure had done particularly well with his selection. The hotel phone rang and it was sweet Cindy.

"Commander Todd, even though it's Friday I've been able to get an Air France flight tonight from London City at eight-fifteen. Would that do?"

"Brilliant, thank you, book it."

"Right... hold the phone will you?" she said brightly. Thirty seconds later she was back.

"Flight all booked with Sunday return—*two* tickets to Toulon—see you at the airport at seven-thirty!"

CHAPTER TEN

We landed at Toulon Hyeres at ten-fifteen and grabbed a taxi to our hotel. Cindy had booked us into Grand Dauphine, a nice, small establishment smack in the middle of the old part of town. Separate rooms of course.

We were hungry, and fortunately there were plenty of cafes and bars all just a short walk from the hotel. A charming little restaurant right around the corner took care of that for us. After a pleasurable dinner, we arranged to meet in the lobby at eight-thirty in the morning, and retired for the night.

Saturday dawned bright, blue, and clear ... a perfect Mediterranean sunrise. I'd slept reasonably well but the hotel was noisy at times. So many young people about—don't they *ever sleep?* Maybe I was beginning to get old.

Before leaving London I'd called the head of the local constabulary, Capitaine Gerard Martin, who had promised to follow up on our earlier enquiry after Connolly. We were to meet him at the station at nine o'clock. After breakfast, Cindy and I met in the lobby as arranged, and we set off on foot for the Gendarmerie in Rue Vincent Allegre.

I marvelled at the beauty of the old city— typically French, lots of three and four-storey buildings with iron-lace balconies. Our walk down the narrow streets and laneways, and across a park for five or six blocks to the station, made me feel good; alive. It had a really romantic vibe; sensual even!

Capitaine Martin greeted us with a "bonjour, comment allez-vouz?"

"Capitaine bonjour, très bien thank you." replied Cindy. I had no idea what they were saying, but it seemed to me perfect French. She was talented.

He ushered us into his office, an unremarkable room in an unremarkable building considering the architecture we'd just witnessed. He then filled us in, thankfully in English, on their tracking of Connolly. Cindy appeared to take notes.

Apparently Connolly had moved into the Toulon area about five years earlier. "That would fit," I explained, "because that would be about when he was released from Wandsworth."

"Five years is quite a stretch ... what did your Mr Connolly do to earn his prison term?" the Capitaine asked.

I briefed him on Connolly's background, the bogus international loans, and the vast sums of money sucked from borrowers in the process. And that some of those borrowers had chased Connolly for their money back— hence the jail stint.

I explained that until his trial, Connolly had maintained he owned an estate in Kent and a villa in Tuscany. His sentencing judge decreed these were fanciful—he owned nothing, and had never had anything of the sort. I told him also of my doubt about the judge's findings—maybe he didn't own the properties, but I believed Connolly must have had a connection to money somewhere.

I then covered the three murders in the last week in London, and how the only connection we could establish between them was a common interest in Connolly. That two of them were the people mostly responsible for Connolly being put in the slammer. And that was why we were here. "So Capitaine, have you found anything of interest for us?" I asked.

"I've had one of my men quietly following him for a couple of days," replied Martin. "He lives an expensive lifestyle it seems; he has quite an impressive villa in Sanary-Sur-Mer around the coast from here—and drives a newish Mercedes. He belongs to a yacht club nearby, and by all accounts dines out regularly."

I clarified that at this point, we just wanted to talk to him... to try and establish any potential link to the murders... but that I was unsure of the best way to proceed. I had to come up with a story, some angle of approach.

"Well," said the Capitaine, "one other thing we do know about Mr Connolly is that he appears very taken by beautiful women. The younger the better I understand. There is a market in Sanary-Sur-Mer each day—so it will be on now until about lunchtime. Lots of locals attend."

"Yes, and your point is?" I asked.

"Well, if he *is* at the market," said Capitaine Martin smiling and nodding directly at Cindy, "I believe you have *the perfect bait sitting right there.*"

Chapter Eleven

C indy and I left Capitaine Martin and set off on foot back to our hotel. We reached the Dauphine and my body demanded caffeine. I grabbed a map of the surrounding towns from the hotel reception and we made a beeline for a nearby patisserie.

We studied the map for maybe half an hour—clearly we'd need our own vehicle for this expedition. Cindy dialled a local car rental and arranged for one to be collected in an hour.

Capitaine Martin's homework on Connolly was certainly thorough. His villa appeared to be right at the southernmost tip of the Sanary-Sur-Mer peninsula. I asked the waiter how long it would take to get to the Sanary markets. He thought maybe twenty minutes . . . normally . . . but as it was Saturday morning it might take an hour.

Too much driving. Backwards and forwards from Toulon would eat up our time. "See if you can find a room for us in Sanary, and I'll fix the account here," I said to Cindy, as I headed back to our hotel.

Ten minutes later she joined me in the lobby. "I've got us into a place which should make life easier—Hotel de la Tour—looks okay, and it's right on the Quai next to the markets." We collected our bags and strolled the four blocks to the car rental office. The day was getting hot.

The paperwork was ready when we arrived. I did the usual signing and handed over the credit card—and Cindy grabbed the keys. "You don't know your way around here," she laughed. "I'll drive."

We stepped out on the pavement and Cindy motioned towards a blue Audi A5 Cabriolet. "This will be us." The girl certainly had style—I hoped the hotel would be this good. She put the top down, slipped the fun-machine into gear, and gently wound out through the narrow streets of Toulon onto the A50.

I was glad she was driving; I still had to formulate this plan . . . the path to Connolly's door. This would give me some thinking time. And she certainly seemed at ease with right-hand-side road rules.

Half-an-hour later we were on the Bandol road, but nowhere near Sanary markets. The waiter in Toulon was right—*everyone* wanted to come here on Saturday morning and we were in the middle of it. So we snaked our way along in the Mediterranean heat, catching glimpses of the fabulous waterway here and there.

Finally we reached the Sanary-Sur-Mer village, after what seemed like all morning. We found a park about two blocks from the hotel and decided to walk. Cafes lined the harbour-front and I was starving, so we grabbed an outside table at the Bar des Sport, looking over the little port. The markets were winding down but there were still plenty of people around, and this would give us a chance to get our bearings.

We sat for maybe an hour and a half, watching the human movement. Everyone seemed to be on holiday, with boats bobbing and clanging at the dock nearby. People are so interesting to watch—I found myself wondering what they were *really* all doing here?

Still, no sign of Connolly—but then it had been ten years and maybe I wouldn't recognise him.

We decided to book into the hotel and then check out the territory. Maybe locate Connolly's villa ... see if we could find anything on his movements in the last week. I paid for lunch and we strolled along the sidewalk, past the now emptying restaurants and bars.

A man sitting alone at a table stood up quickly, half-turned to leave, and his right shoulder clipped Cindy at the elbow, sending her shoulder bag flying onto the pavement. "Excuses mademoiselle," he said, bending to retrieve Cindy's bag and barely looking up, "je suis désolé."

I moved back to my right ready to take this bloke out ... force of habit I guess. He was only slightly built, perhaps about five six or seven, and balding with a ring of closely cropped grey hair. About mid-sixties but it was difficult to tell ... his back was to me and he was moving on. It had all happened in one smooth, fast movement it seemed.

"You all right?" I asked. "What did he say?"

"I'm fine, no damage, I think he just didn't see me and he apologised," she said, reorganising her hair and clothing. We kept on walking, but something was eating away in the back of my mind. Some familiar feeling.

We reached the car and collected our bags—parking was tight so we left the car where it was—and headed over to the hotel.

"Bonjour madame, vous avez une réservation?" the elderly man at reception asked Cindy. I assumed he must have been the owner.

"Oui," she replied, "in the name of Todd. Commander Todd of the Australian Federal Police."

"Excellent, wonderful to have you here Commander and Mrs Todd," he replied, "this is our last available, however I think you will find it acceptable," handing the keys to Cindy. "Top floor, harbour view, *one superior suite for two.*"

CHAPTER TWELVE

We climbed the three floors to our room in silence; no lift meant this could be wearing. It was worth the climb . . . the view was straight from a travel brochure. Windows opening onto the bay, boats coming and going below, and off to our left a view along the quay where we had just eaten, and where Cindy had her brush with the elderly man.

"So, Mrs Todd," I said smiling, "only one room, eh? I guess we'll have to work out the sleeping arrangements later. By the way, we've been working together for three or four days now, and I don't even know your real surname."

"Carter," laughed Cindy, "but that's not important. And as for sleeping, well I'm happy to share. Maybe we could top to toe."

I was becoming aroused just listening to her ... never mind the visual impact. Five feet eight, perfect olive skin, the biggest brown eyes I've ever seen and short-cropped blonde hair. All on top of a fabulously trim body. But there was work to be done. It was still only mid-afternoon and we needed to find something on Connolly.

I suggested we take a drive. Maybe we could catch sight of him, or with more luck, run into him. Maybe even *have a word*.

We jumped into the blue convertible and set off along Bd des Ercoles and Chemin de la Condouliere following the bay all the way down to its southernmost tip. The houses grew progressively grander and the views more expansive. We passed by a yacht club ... I guessed that must have been Connolly's watering hole.

His villa was in the Chemin de la Gardiole, a long, waterfront street lined with vast private estates. Connolly's was right near the end, down a secluded private drive and perched high on a cliff overlooking the expanse of ocean. We could risk driving down it, but I didn't want to startle him.

"Park here," I said to Cindy indicating a space about twenty yards past Connolly's entrance, "and I'll walk down. See if I can spot him. But keep the motor running in case we need a fast getaway. He may not be *thrilled* to see me."

I moved as quickly and quietly as I could down the concrete drive. It seemed to be about fifty yards to some impressive metal gates, and was lined with an occasional tree and plenty of bushes maybe ten feet high, so that gave me some cover.

I was about halfway down when the gates started to open. That was looking good ... I might be able to get right up to the house. Then I heard the growl of an engine starting. I couldn't see anything, but the motor quickly revved to screaming pitch ... like being trackside at Formula 1.

In about three seconds the car was bolting toward me, through the gates. A black Mercedes convertible, tyres screeching and smoking, and he *wasn't* trying to miss. For a split second I stared straight at the driver, then jumped hard into a bush and felt the pain of thorns in my back, ripping my flesh. I grabbed for my gun to take a shot, but the car disappeared, turning sharp left onto the street. A moment later there was a crunch, and more screeching of tyres. I ran as fast as I could to the top of the drive.

By the time I reached Cindy, she was out of the car looking at the damage. "You okay?" I asked breathlessly.

"I'm fine," she reassured me, "but he came out of there like a maniac... just didn't see me, so we've swapped a bit of body-paint."

"Well, two good things I guess," I said, "I got a quick look at him and that was Connolly all right, so he knows we're here. Strange thing though—I could swear that was the same old guy who ran into you at the restaurant earlier."

CHAPTER
THIRTEEN

There was no telling where Connolly might be now, so I would have to hope I could find him tomorrow. He knew I was here and he obviously didn't want to talk—just eliminate me.

I took the opportunity of the leisurely drive to call Sally back in Sydney. She *should* be at home now—it was still early morning. But no answer, and the call went through to message bank. Something seemed wrong— was she deliberately avoiding me?

By the time we reached the hotel, dusk was settling in. Street lights were coming on, and the quay along the waterfront was coming to life with early-evening diners. I headed for the shower; it had been a hot day, particularly combined with the sweat-inducing, adrenaline rush of almost being run down.

I stood under the steaming water, reflecting on the events of the past few hours. I could, of course, enlist the help of Capitaine Martin, and simply go back and arrest Connolly for assault, or possibly attempted murder. After all, I was here on official police business and Connolly should not be trying to run down anyone, copper or not. But he would clam right up if local police were involved. Best use his rush of blood for my *own* benefit, I decided.

Something touched me lightly between the shoulder blades and I stiffened a little.

"You've got a couple of nasty wounds there Commander," purred the gentle tones of Cindy as she ran her hand down my back. "Why don't you let me fix them for you?"

I turned around slowly. She stepped in under the cascading water, her breasts pressing hard against my stomach. A surge of passion swelled right through me, from my feet to the top of my head. I shuddered slightly as I bent down and our lips briefly touched. She tasted of strawberry-flavoured lip-gloss. I licked her lips lightly, again. We kissed deeply this time, tongues furiously competing. Hers felt like velvet. She pulled her body in hard against me.

Her hand brushed lightly against the inside of my thigh, once, and then again a little higher, firmer. I shuddered again. I reached down, and gently lifted her up so I could stare at that heavenly face. She wrapped her legs around me and pushed against the shower wall. It was such a small cubicle, we could barely fit in there together.

I stepped out of the shower and carried her, long legs still wrapped around my waist, both of us dripping wet. I could feel her hot breath on my neck, her head resting lightly on my shoulder, as we slowly made our way to the bed. We pressed together ... hard.

I determined to take my time ... make this last ... to prove just how powerful I was. My mind flipped to an old football match ... that was how I slowed down. But she wouldn't wait, and she was too strong. She was in charge ... this was her domain ... and a final thrust of her hips, and the rake of her nails down my back, confirmed it.

Our panting, clammy bodies rolled apart ... drying on the sheets ... a cool, salty breeze from the harbour trickling over us. The shower hissed loudly in the bathroom. For a while we just lay there, staring at the slowly turning ceiling fan.

I finally looked over at her. She smiled gently. "I don't know what you just did, but thank you," I said, "I think those wounds are beginning to heal nicely."

CHAPTER FOURTEEN

Sunday morning dawned the usual bright blue, and warm. I got up from the bed as quietly as I could, without disturbing the sleeping beauty next to me.

We hadn't made it very far last night after our first love-making encounter. Couldn't get enough of each other, so we stayed in. No food, nothing. Just more love-making, or sex. Probably both!

I peered out the window across the harbour front. Cafes were setting up, and the first of the morning diners were making their selections. I realised we hadn't eaten anything substantial since lunchtime yesterday. No wonder I was ravenous. I headed to the shower—maybe this time I might get to finish it.

Cindy appeared when I was halfway done, but I turned her around and smacked her lightly on the bottom. "Not enough room—I'll call you when I'm through."

Forty-five minutes later we were strolling along the waterfront, making our own selection from the cafes, and found one with a view straight out past the boats. After pancakes and eggs and pastries and two cups of coffee, we decided to walk it off around the quaint Sanary-Sur-Mer shops which lined the tiny, cobbled alleys behind the main cafe strip.

We walked for two or three blocks and were about to cross Rue Andre Tassy, when I spotted a familiar looking vehicle parked about forty yards away, in a parking lot at the end of the street. "When Connolly hit the convertible, what part of his copped it?" I asked.

"Right-side I think—yes, I was parked on the right and he hit my left side, with his front-right."

I pointed to the black Mercedes. "Let's have a closer look."

We moved along the footpath, trying to look as much like unconcerned tourists as possible. With my size though, it's difficult to be unobtrusive about anything. Ten yards from the SL 63, and we could see just the evidence we were after . . . sure enough the front-right guard showed the tell-tale signs of yesterday's impact, and a nicely grafted strip of blue duco from the Audi as well.

I glanced up and down the street, but there was no obvious sign of Connolly. He had to be here *somewhere*—it seemed to be a regular haunt for him.

"Can you whistle?" I asked.

"You mean like this?" said Cindy popping two index fingers in her mouth and emitting a low wolf-whistle. Why would I have expected any less?

"Perfect," I said, "now we'll cut through to the next block—plenty of shops there. I'll take this side and you check the far side. If you see him, do nothing, just whistle me and wait till I get there. I'll do the same. Don't get too near him."

We slipped down the short alley to Rue Barthelemey de Don, and set off in opposite directions. I'd barely moved more than twenty paces, when I heard a shrill blast from further down the street. I looked across the top of the few window shoppers, and could see Cindy, backed-up against a whitewashed wall, her arm in the air waving frantically for me to come.

"Christ," I muttered, did she need to whistle so loudly? They'd hear it in Toulon, not to mention attracting the attention of everyone in the vicinity. I moved quickly across the narrow street, trying not to look like I was in a maniacal hurry, until I was about two shops short of Cindy, who was still backed against the wall.

She put her hand up indicating for me to stop, and pointed excitedly at the entrance of a small boutique. I eased back a couple of feet, up against a neighbouring shop. At least here he couldn't see me until he was on the footpath.

We waited for maybe four or five minutes, but it seemed like half an hour. Passers-by must have wondered what in the hell we were doing, judging from their animated finger pointing and conversations.

Then in a flash he appeared. Dressed in jeans and a black cotton jacket, he turned right as he exited the boutique, and caught sight of Cindy a few feet away.

"What the fuck do you want?" Connolly hissed at her, as he turned abruptly back to his left.

I took two giant steps before he could do his about-face, grabbed his left shoulder and ripped his right arm around behind him, then face-slammed him into the shop wall. The small, brightly wrapped package he'd just bought flew into the gutter. I'm guessing it was glass, judging from the distinct smashing sound.

"Paul Connolly I believe?" I asked, keeping his face pressed firmly against the brickwork.

"Depends who's asking."

"Detective Commander Ashley Todd, Australian Federal Police—*I thought we should catch up for old time's sake.*"

CHAPTER FIFTEEN

With Cindy following behind, I led Connolly across the street and into the small alley which connected to the car park, and his damaged Mercedes. Now we were away from the passing human traffic, we could have a *meaningful* discussion.

He was indignant at being so roughly manhandled, especially in public. "Disgraceful treatment of an elderly gentleman," were his exact words. I explained to him that 'elderly gentlemen' did not crash into ladies on the footpath, then scurry off like a shit-scared hare. Nor did they attempt to run down a police officer acting in the line of duty. This latter action, I further explained, could be considered attempted murder.

The threat of such charge seemed to focus his attention. "I haven't seen you for ten years Commander, and hoped I never would again. But I'm clean, I've done my time, and I don't intend to do any more. When I ran into your lady friend, that was an accident and I apologise. When you turned up at my house, I had no idea why you were there, but with my background ... you understand, I get very nervous. So I panicked and decided to skip. What is it you want?"

"We've had three people murdered in London in the past week. Two men and a woman. Have you been to London during that time?" I asked.

"No, I have not."

"You sure ... we can check?"

"Absolutely positive."

I decided we should continue this conversation somewhere more comfortable. Three people standing around in a back alley might attract more attention than necessary. However I didn't want Connolly doing a runner, as this appeared to be his specialty.

"We'll move to the cafe on the corner, but I'm going to cuff you to me. Leave your jacket on and no one will notice. I just want you to hang around and answer *all* my questions, until I say you can leave." We shuffled off in a strange sort of huddle, Cindy and I on each side of him, but once we were seated he seemed to relax more. It did feel strangely uncomfortable though, to have him sitting so close.

"As I said," I continued, "three people murdered and they all have a connection to you."

"W-what connection," he stammered, "who are they?"

"The two men were instrumental in convicting you—Terry Walker and Andrew Lau. The woman was Walker's lover—Juanita Sanchez."

Connolly put his head down, and closed his eyes as though in prayer. He sat that way for a couple of minutes, saying nothing but rocking gently back and forth. "Sorry," he said, "force of habit. Whenever I get under stress I use that to relax. Just the mention of their names stirs me up. But the woman—*never* heard of her."

"Tell me," I said, changing the subject, "when you were released you were broke. Now you live in a villa that would be the envy of most people—must be worth a few mill. You drive a flash car—which has now been used to cause grief to my car—and you don't appear to work. How do you pay for it?"

"House belongs to a friend. Let's me stay there rent free, and he owns the car too."

"Why does he let you stay there?" I asked.

"Because we've been long-term buddies, and I guess he felt sorry for me after the prison stint."

That seemed unlikely . . . far too generous.

"So who owns the house?"

"My mate's name is Dave, but he has a company which owns the house."

"Does *Dave* have another name," I asked sarcastically, "and what company owns the house?"

"Not sure of his other name. Company is called Soacha Capital I think." Cindy was taking notes again, so I had him spell it, just to make sure.

"You must be close buddies," I replied, "when you can't even remember his name. We'll check this Soacha Capital. So, if you weren't in London, where were you?"

"I was here, all week."

"Anyone verify that . . . you know, an alibi?"

"N–no, I don't think so. I was home all that time, and there's no one else, you see . . ."

"So you know nothing of these murders— of Sanchez, Walker, or Lau?"

Connolly put his head down again and rocked. "N–nothing at all."

I took a sheet of paper from Cindy's note- pad and wrote out a statement.

"Right," I said, "we're going to check all this, and if I find you've been bullshitting me, I'll come back and personally carry you back into the slammer. And I'll add *attempted murder of a cop* to the list."

"N–no bullshit—honest."

"I think we're done here," I said as solemnly as possible, "in a moment I'll let you go. But first you can sign this," sliding the sheet of paper under his nose.

"W–what is it?" he said craning his neck over the paper. The stammering was getting worse.

"I'm on a plane back to London this evening. This is an irrevocable undertaking that you will pay for the damage to our rental car. That's the least you can offer to do. Plus, they might have some chance of finding you." Connolly hurriedly signed the statement.

"Now you can go," I said unlocking the cuffs.

And off he scurried across the street, a little old man disappearing into the alley, *just like a shit-scared hare.*

CHAPTER SIXTEEN

We spent the next few hours trawling the little shops of Sanary-Sur-Mer. Just a couple of tourists.

I bought Cindy a ring, a bright yellow and blue fake stone, but the colours seemed perfect for this town. And she bought me a pair of socks—blue and white stripes—I guess she thought they looked a bit nautical. A quick bite of late lunch and it was back to the hotel to pack.

I kept thinking of my conversation with Connolly. He was very nervous—I would say too nervous for a man with nothing to hide. Sure, five years in the nick for a man his age would probably play havoc with his system. Particularly after a life of first-class global jet-setting. But I still had nothing else on him, *yet*.

Despite it being Sunday afternoon, I phoned Inspector McClure and briefed him on our, *little*, progress. He seemed pleased enough to get my call. He had no updates but his team continued to scour the area where Juanita Sanchez was found, and he expected a report from his sergeant in the morning.

I filled him in on our run-in, literally, with Connolly; on Connolly's supposed benefactor Dave, with no other name, and the villa held in the name of Soacha Capital. McClure agreed to check out this company, and promised to have some answers the next day. We arranged to meet at his office at midday.

We still had an hour or more drive to the airport, and check in was six-thirty... the time to depart was fast approaching. I took a long, last look from the hotel room window at the beautiful harbour. I was so happy with Cindy, but felt a touch low to be leaving. Cindy put her arms around me, and we kissed passionately. Life has a way of delivering the strangest things, I reflected. I had come for Connolly, found him and got nothing much. But I hadn't come for anything else, and found something totally unexpected.

We jumped in the convertible and headed for the airport, Cindy at the wheel as usual. Shit, I thought, I should try Sally again. I'd forgotten all about her since the evening before. I dialled the number ... but something inside me *hoped she wouldn't answer.*

CHAPTER
SEVENTEEN

P aul Connolly locked his black convertible inside his garage, then double-checked to make sure the automatic doors had indeed closed properly. He wanted no more surprises today.

He limped slowly across the double height reception hall to his office, and scanned the video screens which covered the long driveway and automatic front gates. All clear . . . gates securely locked.

He stepped in to the downstairs bathroom and inspected his forehead—quite a graze which had now formed into a decent size lump and bruise. That damn Todd had smacked him so hard into the wall, and he was such a big bastard he probably didn't realise the damage he'd done. And his knee hurt—probably from the same roughing up.

He rummaged through the vanity drawer, found a couple of paracetamol and a Sertraline, and gulped them down together. *That* should settle the nerves.

He gingerly made his way to the back of the house, but he just couldn't enjoy the view. Too stressful. These people were on to him; he needed a drink, badly. He poured a double scotch with one block of ice. Then he sat on the big blue sofa, staring out at the ocean, but seeing nothing. Tears began to blur his vision.

Why did my life have to look like this, he wondered? Once I was a respected lawyer in a major investment bank in New York. A chance meeting a dozen years ago with Dave got me on this path. It all seemed so promising, and then everything collapsed. I did time for five years, *their fucking time*, and still they own me. I don't know how I'm ever going to get away from it.

He threw down the rest of the scotch and grabbed a refill. Gotta make a call. He grabbed the phone, dialled, and took another gulp. A heavily accented voice answered. "Yes?"

"Mr Alvarez this is Paul Connolly," he said slightly nervously, though the pills and liquor were having the desired effect.

"I know," replied Alvarez, "what is your problem?"

"I think they're on to me, for you know the . . . you know doing the j-job."

"Who, *exactly*, is on to you?"

"Commander Todd—he's the one from Australia who put me away before—and that young girl, you know . . ."

"What was he asking?" Alvarez cut in.

"He says Walker and Lau—you know they're the ones who you were going to meet—he says they're dead. And the Sanchez woman too. I don't know anything about fucking killing them . . . except the woman of course . . . but he's roughed me up a bit, and he's a clever big bastard. He won't let go, it'll be just like before . . . ."

"What did you say to him?" Alvarez asked testily.

"N–nothing, told him nothing, said I didn't know anything about any murders, hadn't been to London."

"And he believed you?"

"I think so, he let me go; but he made me sign for smashing up his car."

"*What* car did you smash?"

"H–he came round here looking for me and I took off, but I clipped his wheels in the process. He made me sign something saying I'd pay. I don't think I've left any clues behind, but like I say, he can be relentless and what if he comes back here?"

"Very careless, panicking like that. Keep calm," said Alvarez sternly. "I will have someone collect the car tomorrow, and have it repaired. Say nothing to anyone. And as for this Commander Todd... *I will have him attended to.*"

Chapter Eighteen

The flight back to London went smoothly enough and Cindy and I parted company at the airport with a final kiss. I would see her tomorrow at her office.

Sally had finally answered my call, but I still didn't feel any easier about it. She said she'd been ill, too sick to get out of bed, and she didn't feel much like talking. I promised to try her again in a few days, when she had recovered. Then I headed back to the luxury of Browns Hotel.

Next morning I arrived at McClure's office a little before midday. Cindy was at her desk and I gave her a little smile and a wink. Too many people about, and the last thing I needed was to have rumours flying around the Met about *us*. No need to undermine my professional standing with the chief inspector.

McClure's deputy DI Carty joined us, with a review of information gathered by the various teams. The Marine Support Unit had divers scouring the water within a two hundred yard radius of where Juanita Sanchez was found. They had recovered various items including a crowbar, three car tyres and what appeared to be a rusted part from an old printing press—but no weapon. People ditch some strange shit.

The general duty teams, conducting their door knock, had interviewed an elderly couple who lived at the end of Jamestown Way. They recalled hearing what sounded like a woman yelling. It seemed like it was coming from Riverside Park, just across the road, but only lasted for about thirty seconds. The husband had looked out two or three times after the commotion, but there was no sign of any woman; only, after about five minutes a smallish, older looking man making his way back towards the railway. It was fairly dark and hard to make out much more. He assumed he was just a local resident and thought nothing more of it.

McClure's team had followed up on Soacha Capital and found it was registered in the Cayman Islands.

"Jim, are you able to find who is behind this company?" I asked. "Do you have any contacts in the Caymans?"

"Sure do," replied McClure, "I spent five years in the SCD6, our money laundering unit, and dealt with the Cayman police many times. Inspector Joel Roberts is an old friend—I'll give him a call."

We agreed to break for a couple of hours and reconvene at three o'clock. I dropped in on Cindy on my way past. "How about lunch?"

"Fabulous," she smiled, "I'm famished."

"Can you check something for me?" She nodded. "Can you Google the word Soacha and see what it brings up? I'll meet you in, say, ten at Starbucks on Victoria Street."

I ducked back to see McClure, who was on the phone. He held one finger up indicating for me to wait, and that he'd only be a minute. "That was a quick lunch," he said on hanging up.

"Sorry to appear to pressure you, but I wondered if you'd had a chance to call your man in the Caymans yet?"

"That was him. I've given him the brief and he'll get onto it straight away. He has a contact in the general registry there, a woman called Marlene Rix who's been there forever and knows everything, *apparently*, and he'll get back to me. Should have the answer when you get back."

"Thanks mate," I said and turned for the lift. I had a hunch that, finally, we could start to put some of the pieces together.

CHAPTER
NINETEEN

I arrived at the coffee shop and Cindy was already seated at a table in the back left corner. We ordered two coffees and two baguettes, toasted.

"I've been wanting to tell you that I enjoyed the last two days more than anything else in the last two years. But I don't know anything about you," I said.

"I enjoyed it too, but I don't think there's much to tell," she replied casually, "what do you want to know?"

"The usual—where you come from, what you've done, what made you join the Met. All the sort of things that would interest a police officer," I laughed.

"Oh, I've lived in London all my life—thirty three years—and I had, I guess, a pretty normal upbringing. My father is in business ... he's an importer ... and my mother died a few years ago. She wasn't well for some time. Did law at Kingston University, joined a law firm in the city, then this job as assistant to DCI McClure came up and I jumped at it. Much more interesting solving the riddles of the world. And what about you?"

"Well," I said, trying to choose the right words, "I was born in rural Australia—a small town in the far west of a state called Queensland. Have you heard of it—Queensland that is?"

"I think so," she nodded, "is that what they call the outback?"

"Sure is—miles from anywhere. Australia is a huge country, and mostly empty. Anyway I was found at the entrance of the local hospital, an abandoned baby, and made a State ward. The nurses there named me Ashley but don't ask me why ... I think it's a girlie name. When I was a bit older, maybe four or five, I was adopted by a couple named Todd in Brisbane, which is the state capital. So that's how I got my name."

Cindy sipped her coffee, smiling gently as she took in the story.

"I had a good life with them—they were much older parents and are both now dead. After school I joined the police force and got a law degree—international law was my go— and then a bit later I did a Masters in Forensic Psychology. About ten years ago, while I was still in Queensland, I became involved in this fraud case with Connolly and your boss. Then around eight years ago, the Australian Federal Police head-hunted me and I moved to Sydney. Now I'm here."

The food arrived and we ate in silence for a few minutes.

"Fascinating," she said, "and you have no idea who your real parents are?"

"None at all, except a while ago I had a DNA test done—searching for my biological parents under freedom of information; that sort of thing. Anyway, they found I had abo-riginal blood, but no luck with my parents. I sometimes feel it's hard to settle down— maybe that's the reason, I don't know."

"Well, whatever the background, it pro-duced a magnificent physical specimen," she laughed.

"Luck of the draw I guess, but I must admit it has come in handy playing football when I was younger, and catching outlaws and villians now. Speaking of which—I nearly forgot—did you find anything on Soacha?"

"Yes, but not much—it's a suburb of Bogota, in Colombia."

"Colombia, how very interesting." I glanced at the coffee-shop clock. "Hell, we'd better get back. *Can't keep VIP's waiting.*"

Y ou two been on a date?" asked
McClure. I checked my watch and saw
it was ten past three.

"Sorry Jim," I said, "we just had to run a
probe on a couple of things."

McClure then went over the conversation
he'd had with his counterpart, Inspector
Roberts, of the Cayman Island police. Soacha
Capital was an exempt company in the
Caymans, with a registered office in George
Town, and a sole director, one David Perez.

Robert's contact in the registry, Marlene
Rix, knew Perez quite well. He was a lawyer
who came to the Caymans four or five years
ago. His reputation was a bit dusty around the

edges, but he kept a low profile due to *unforeseen circumstances* in recent times.

"I think we are beginning to see a pattern here," I said. "It might be just a coincidence, but these people, except our two initial victims, have something in common. They even share it with the company which owns Connolly's villa."

"And that is?" asked McClure.

"Their names—Sanchez, Perez—they're Colombian. And Soacha is a city in Colombia. There *has* to be a connection."

McClure leaned back in his chair, looked at the ceiling, and let out a long, low whistle.

"I don't know why Connolly would be tied up with them—that is, with people from Colombia—but everything about Connolly's past is strange," I continued. "I've a feeling that if we're going to get to the bottom of this, I need to get to the Caymans and see what I can find from this Perez. If we keep pushing hard enough, eventually someone will crack."

"I agree Ash, but we both know that this is starting to enter damned dangerous territory. I've spent a shitload of time in the specialist agencies here, and I tell you, these Colombians will do *anything* if you look like you are upsetting their turf."

"Maybe so Jim, but remember ten years ago our Connolly investigation just sort of ran out. He was the end of the line, so off he went to the slammer. I always felt it was incomplete—something was missing, but we just couldn't get to it. I have a gut feeling that we might be just stumbling into *it* now. And, the truth is, the same gut feeling tells me I've got to try and finish *it*."

McClure buzzed Cindy on his intercom. "Could you book Commander Todd on the first available flight tomorrow morning, to New York, with a connecting flight to George Town, Cayman Islands? Also, he'll be needing some accommodation."

"Yes sir, any return date?"

"I hope so, but not now."

We waited in silence, staring out at the neighbouring buildings, until Cindy buzzed back. "All booked on British Airways from Heathrow at 8:00 a.m. tomorrow sir, and accommodation at the Ritz Carlton on Seven Mile Beach."

I stood to leave and DCI McClure grabbed my hand, shook it firmly, and put his arm around me. "For God's sake be careful Ash. As a consummate copper I hate saying it, but I'd rather *fail* to solve this—and have you back in one piece."

"I'll be careful... don't worry... and I fully intend to return in the state you now see me. One more thing—the bodies of Walker and Lau—where are they now?"

"We released them today. Walker's was sent to his family in New Zealand. His daughter I think. Lau's wife had contacted us from Hong Kong, so he's gone there. Why do you ask?"

"Not sure, but sometimes following the body can be beneficial. I'll call you from the Caymans."

I strode out of McClure's office through the vast open plan arrangement, with constables preoccupied at computer screens. Strange I thought, Cindy wasn't at her desk. I turned into the vestibule which housed the lifts, and there she stood. A quick check behind—no-one else about—only the CCTV cameras, but what the hell.

I bent down and kissed her firmly. "Got to go—look after yourself—I'll be back soon."

She gave me a half-smile. "Be careful," she whispered and turned towards the offices. I could have sworn she was crying.

CHAPTER
TWENTY-ONE

B ig Ben struck eight p.m. as the black Maybach turned off Piccadilly and slid along Albemarle Street, Mayfair. Ernesto Alvarez sat in the back, earphones on, soaking in Mahler's Symphony number four, contemplating how this might play out. His importing business in the United Kingdom had operated, mostly without interference, for more than thirty years. Occasionally someone had to be paid to ensure the supply chain was unhindered, but to him that was just a cost of business.

His preferred commodities... heroin, cocaine, and more recently, ice... had found an ever expanding market, and created an enviable lifestyle for him and his family.

Except when someone had to be terminated. That part of the lifestyle may not be enviable, but from time to time it was necessary. The mood enhancement industry, as he referred to it, occasionally demanded nothing less. His personal motto... *Eliminate Your Foe, Or Perish*... sometimes left a sour taste, but had proved effective. Of course there was a pay-off... *obscene wealth*!

This time though, was more troubling than usual. Police officers who found their way into his world could usually be seen off... for a fee. Just a cost of business. Or they were actively recruited to be part of it. This time, he doubted either approach would work.

He reflected on the more recent disposals, the two would-be borrowers from long ago who had resurfaced—Mr Walker and Mr Lau—and the woman, Juanita Sanchez. Lau, of course, was more than just a borrower. He was potentially useful. But he had brought in Walker... more baggage from the past... and the demands started. That was over the top!

Then there was Juanita. Beautiful Juanita... best tits in town! But she knew too much; too close to both sides of his business, and that was always dangerous. Pity though, that he had to use Connolly to dispose of her. He always seemed slightly mentally unstable, but he and his colleagues owed him. Connolly had taken the rap, and they had guaranteed to support him. Just a cost of business.

Alvarez instructed his driver to stop the limousine about twenty yards past Browns Hotel. The two men strode to the lobby—the driver indicating to the concierge they would only be five minutes—then rode the lift to room 303. The driver knocked four times sharply. There was no answer. Strange, thought Alvarez. He nodded to the driver who knocked again four times. No answer. They turned and re-entered the lift.

"I will return to the car. You check his whereabouts with reception," Alvarez instructed his driver.

Alvarez waited, seated in the rear and resumed his Mahler concert. The driver slipped into the front seat a few minutes later. "Well," asked Alvarez, "what news?"

"Gone sir," replied the driver, glancing in the rear view mirror, "checked out one hour ago."

CHAPTER TWENTY-TWO

The cab pulled into the entrance to the Sheraton Skyline hotel in Bath Road opposite Heathrow airport. When people tell me to "be careful" I usually dismiss it as unnecessary worry. Either that, or it's a threat, so I deal with them on the spot. But Cindy's gentle words kept playing on my mind. And McClure had also said "be careful."

I didn't know what she meant; maybe it was just a saying of hers like some people say "keep well", or plain old "good luck." Still, I needed to be at the airport by six-thirty the next morning, and that meant a four-thirty start from my city base. Don't like those hours much, so I decided to move on to somewhere closer to my flight—and grab some extra sleep.

I checked in and put a call into Sally. No answer—this was concerning, particularly if she had been sick. But I guessed she was already at work. Then I rummaged through my luggage for my Rolodex. I'd had this old thing for twenty years or more, from my early policing days, and wrote every phone number of importance at any given time, in it.

I slid the tab to the letter L, flipped it open, and slowly trawled through the list of names and numbers. Some were pretty hard to read, so many changes and cross outs, but I finally found it—Andrew Lau—and a Hong Kong phone number. I had no idea whether this would be current—it was at least ten years old—but I thought it was worth a try.

I dialled the number and waited as it made the familiar international dialling noises. A female voice answered . . . "Wai."

"Hello," I said brightly, "is that Mrs Lau?"

"Yes," she replied, sounding somewhat nervous, but with an impeccably British accent, "who is this?"

I explained to her who I was, my past association with her late husband, and offered my condolences. She recalled me from the previous case, and her tone became more relaxed. I then explained my new involvement, investigating his murder.

"So Mrs Lau, did you know your husband was coming to London on business?"

"Of course," she replied, "we keep an apartment there. He has been doing business in London for many years."

"Did you know who he intended to meet?"

"Well, I know he spoke a number of times to that Mr Connolly, the chap who failed to deliver the money before, but I don't think he was meeting him. I really can't recall, but I have a feeling it was maybe Mr Sands. You remember him? He was Mr Connolly's representative, in Australia, for the money."

I assured her I certainly did remember Sands. "But it can't be him ... he's no longer with us either."

"Well ... then possibly it could have been Mr Alvarez."

I was gobsmacked. *Alvarez*! "Are we talking about Ernesto Alvarez?" I asked cautiously.

"I believe that is his name."

"So your husband knew Alvarez before this meeting?"

"Oh, yes," she replied, "he knew him. I don't know the details, but he used to say *they were going into business together. Partners!*"

CHAPTER TWENTY-THREE

I t was seven thirty five p.m. when I landed at Owen Roberts International Airport on Grand Cayman—right on time with American Airlines. All day spent as a guest of the airline industry is boring . . . time passes so slowly . . . but at least I had a chance to think about developments in the murders to date.

We had Walker and Lau both with an old connection to Connolly, but absolutely no clue why they were together now. They both went to a meeting at The Landmark Hotel on Marylebone Road—but we don't know who they met. Maybe they met with Alvarez, or maybe even with Connolly. We know there was a woman present, whom we now know was Juanita Sanchez.

From the forensic evidence found in the bed, we know she had sex with *someone*, at present unknown. We know Sanchez had been living with Walker. But why would she attend his murder? Was she a willing partici-pant? And who was she screwing *behind his back*?

Whatever the answers to all our un-knowns were, it was obvious the old con-nection to Connolly from ten years earlier had been reignited. In that investigation, we hit a brick wall once we got to Connolly. The trail died with him. This time though, there seemed to be more players involved.

Connolly was now living the high life, despite his lack of resources, in a villa appar-ently owned by a Cayman Island company. A company with a Colombian name, and con-trolled by a David Perez.

And now the possibility was that one of our victims, Lau, had prior dealings with one Ernesto Alvarez. I shuddered when I thought of him. Czar of the drug trade in the United Kingdom. Ruthless, violent, and extremely wealthy. His name had appeared on a number of major cases I had been involved in over the past twenty years. No-one could ever touch him.

I took a cab to the hotel Cindy had booked for me, checked-in and ordered room service. Tomorrow I would meet with McClure's mate, Inspector Roberts, and see what pieces of the puzzle he could shed some light on.

In the meantime, whoever the unknown male was in The Landmark room was obviously critical to our case. It occurred to me DNA evidence might be the only way we could prove his identity. If it was Connolly, that was easy. If The Yard didn't already have it on file, I knew where he was, and I could get it.

But if it was Alvarez, that was different! I imagined he didn't scare easily, if at all. I had no idea how I could get anything from him— without risking my own death. At that point I felt I'd be safer standing naked in the midst of a Cayman hurricane.

CHAPTER
TWENTY-FOUR

I had breakfast in my room at the Ritz Carlton, overlooking the waters of the Caribbean. The brochures were right—everything was very, very blue. There was no doubt, this case was certainly taking me to some exotic locations. Shame I couldn't spend more time in each of them. Or at least come for pleasure, not work.

I took a cab into George Town and met with Inspector Roberts, who occupied a pleasant, but unremarkable office on the first floor of the Royal Cayman Islands Police Service in Elgin Street. A tall good-looking man in his mid-fifties, he had been a friend of McClure's for thirty years, mostly from their work together in financial and organised crime.

"I landed at an airport last night with the same surname as yours," I said light-heartedly, hoping to establish an easy-going rapport, "I don't suppose you own it?"

"As a matter of fact," he said straight-faced, "it *is* named after my family. And yes, I collect annual rental from all air traffic movement."

"I'm sorry," I said blushing slightly, "I wasn't meaning to be rude." Better leave the comedy routine to somewhere safer, I thought.

"Don't worry," he said throwing his head back and laughing loudly, "I have *no* connection with it. People sometimes ask, so I have a standard reply. I just like to see the effect it has on them. Now, what can I do to help with your investigation?"

I explained what we had uncovered to date, but tying up a connection between the individuals was proving a problem. Any connection was based purely on old associations. There seemed to be no evidence I could put my finger on, which linked any of them to the murders. The company, Soacha Capital, was of interest, and particularly the man who appeared to be behind it, David Perez.

Roberts suggested I might like to meet with his friend, Marlene Rix. Marlene had worked for two decades in the General Registry office on Goring Avenue. Not only could she bring up background on companies and individuals in the Caymans, but she had developed a network of people who knew 'behind the scenes' information. He had found her knowledge invaluable in helping solve cases.

The Caymans' lure as a centre of financial discretion and secrecy was very appealing ... to both legitimate and illegitimate business dealings. Hell ... that might be the *only* reason it existed. Roberts' task, of course, was concerned with the illegitimate ones, and that's where Marlene came in. What was *not* written down, and recorded, was what he needed to know, and Marlene's contacts seemed able to supply it. "She knows shit about people they, themselves don't know," Roberts said, laughing again.

He picked up the phone and dialled. "Marlene, Joel here, how goes it?" They had a polite chitchat for a couple of minutes.

"Marlene, I have Commander Todd from the Australian Federal Police here. He's working with an old colleague of mine, Jim McClure, from Scotland Yard. You remember you checked a company Soacha Capital, and its director David Perez, for me?"

Marlene did indeed recall the company. Inspector Roberts suggested she might like to meet with me . . . to discuss her findings in more detail. "Of course," she replied, "send him around."

"You available now?" Roberts asked, turning to me.

"Absolutely—can't think of a better time."

"I'll get a car and driver," Roberts said to Marlene, "he's coming at ya."

CHAPTER
TWENTY-FIVE

The General Registry office, and therefore Marlene Rix, was located in the Citrus Grove building on Goring Avenue. It was only a three or four block drive from Inspector Roberts office. I could have walked it, but Roberts insisted I use his car.

I introduced myself to Ms Rix, a short, plumpish woman in her mid-forties, with short, curly dark hair and no-nonsense, black rimmed spectacles. We shook hands and she ushered me into a small meeting room at the rear of the ground floor. I thanked her for the work she had done, and the information she'd already found on Soacha Capital and David Perez.

"Do you know anything of Mr Perez?" she asked, cutting in quickly.

I assured her I didn't, that his name and his company had only come up last week, in an investigation I was conducting in London and France.

"Commander Todd," she continued, "let me be perfectly frank. I don't know you, and I don't know your colleague Inspector McClure, but I have known Inspector Roberts for a long time and we are good friends. Our friendship is, however, purely professional."

"I understand."

"Whatever I say here, however, is *off* the record. If there is anything you find, from information which I provide, that leads you to a court room—please do not ask that I attend that court room to give evidence. Do I make myself clear?"

"Perfectly," I replied, noting her direct approach. It seemed to me she might view life as if looking down two ramrod straight railroad tracks, and did not veer outside either.

"Many years ago, when I first joined here, the Caymans was *the* place to conduct financial affairs in secret. Then governments became paranoid about the asset protection industry. They started to strip away confidentiality; chip away at established practices. International crime became much more sophisticated ... and is always looking for another home. Alternative jurisdictions opened up worldwide to accommodate them."

"Sure," I agreed, "new and interesting centres opened up everywhere."

"The thing is, Commander, it's not just criminals who want asset protection. There are plenty of people, and corporations, who financially support government. They also wish to conduct their affairs without that same government knowing. As a result, secondary industries began to flourish—a lot of companies and people here were fronts for all sorts of organisations—and none of it was written down. The knowledge of all this was in someone's head, only."

"So where does that place the people I'm interested in?" I asked.

"I'll get to that in a minute. The authorities here set up a division ... it is un-named and officially does not exist. But I have run it for seven or eight years. My job is to know who is behind certain companies, and what they *really* do. We do nothing with the information, unless pressed. It serves as a kind of insurance for the government of the Caymans. That is why whatever I tell you, is for your ears only. Agreed?"

"Agreed."

"The company, Soacha Capital, was established four or five years ago. Its sole director, as you know, is Mr David Perez. Mr Perez is a lawyer who set up a practice here about five years ago. He came here from the States... New Jersey... where he was also a lawyer. I have a long-term contact of mine in New York, who can give you a much more comprehensive background on him."

Marlene Rix went on to describe the legal practice operated by Perez, the type of clientele he represented, his homosexual lifestyle and the type of partners he seemed to favour. At a personal level, there appeared to be little she didn't know, unless she was inventing it. This was obviously all part of the 'insurance' the government liked to hold.

When she had finished her briefing, I thanked her profusely. "I think my next move should be to try and meet Mr Perez; see if he might be more forthcoming than others in his circle."

"I wish you luck with him Commander, but please be careful."

There it was again—another woman telling me to *be careful*. "Any particular reason why I need to be especially careful?"

"Colombians, Commander, to be brutally honest. Not those who visit here. They are, by and large, good people. It's those who use us as a base for their business dealings. They control so much—not just drugs, but money, corporations, governments—their reach is everywhere. Perez is Colombian. His company has a Colombian name. But he is not the ultimate problem. That belongs to the man I believe he really represents—the most brutal of them all—and *that* is why I want you to be careful."

"Thanks for your concern Marlene," I said, "but who might that be?"

Marlene Rix stared straight through me for a moment, looked down at the floor and then lifted her gaze back to mine. *"A Mr Alvarez. Ernesto Alvarez."*

CHAPTER TWENTY-SIX

I sat at the Margaritaville bar opposite the pier, listening to some Jimmy Buffet, sipping a cold beer and watching some twenty-somethings swim up for their, as Jimmy himself might say, favourite concoction. They seemed not to have a care in the world, and I found myself wishing I could be in their shoes.

I thought about Sally. I had been away for over a week, and we had only had one brief conversation in that time. She never seemed to answer—maybe she was sick, but what if it was something more? I guessed it would be about one in the morning back in Sydney, so I made a mental note to call her in six hours.

Marlene Rix was right—if Alvarez was really behind Soacha and David Perez, then I was walking into a veritable snake pit. *Be careful* indeed! Alvarez was not someone I had crossed in my life, except in name and reputation. Funny, I thought, how he was not even on our radar a week ago, and now after a short conversation with the wife of one of our victims, his name seemed to crop up at every turn.

I wanted to talk to Perez but I assumed he would not particularly want to talk to me. In fact, I guessed he would be downright hostile. Therefore I needed a threat to help convince him. Something, other than my physical size, that would make him see the wisdom in at least entering a discussion.

Marlene had mentioned something which piqued my interest—Perez and homosexuality. She must have *something* on him which would be potentially embarrassing, otherwise she would not have brought it up. I gave her a quick call.

"Marlene, in our conversation you mentioned the out-of-hours activities of our mutual friend," I said, deliberately avoiding names for fear of casual eavesdropping.

"Yes, what would you like to know?"

"Anything that might allow me to pressure him—any information that would be sensitive."

"Come to my office again at four-thirty, and we will discuss it." The phone went dead.

I slowly finished another beer, then set off for the leisurely ten-minute walk to the General Registry office. When I arrived Marlene was, again, waiting for me at reception, and ushered me into the same meeting room we'd occupied earlier.

"This information is for you, and you only. Nobody in the Caymans knows of it, except for those involved, my superior and myself."

"Excellent," I said, "what is it?"

"This came to the attention of the Governor, and caused the immediate resignation of the person concerned, described as 'retirement due to family concerns'. For the last two years *Perez has been the lover of the past Chief Justice of the Caymans.*"

CHAPTER
TWENTY-SEVEN

I arrived outside the office of David Perez on Bodden Street, at 9:47 a.m. I had called him after my last conversation the day before with Marlene Rix. The call only lasted a few minutes—I got the distinct impression Perez knew who I was, although he didn't say as much, and that he was none too keen to talk to me.

However, armed with Marlene's 'insurance' ammunition, I suggested that we had items of mutual interest which should be discussed. I don't think he was convinced, but he agreed anyway to a meeting at ten o'clock the next morning. I arrived earlier to try and get an idea of any comings and goings from his office, just in case he may have acquired some outside help.

I had also finally got hold of Sally and we chatted for nearly ten minutes. At least she wasn't ill, but just incredibly busy with her legal work. Maybe that was true, but something still didn't sit well with me—her tone was slightly distant. Perhaps it was just the international call—sometimes the lines make communication slightly difficult—whatever it was, I was left with more niggling questions about our relationship.

I walked up the steps to the first floor of a rundown, two-storey building ... whitish-grey paint flaking from the walls and chipped tiles lining the entrance hall ... which housed the Perez office. It didn't look much like the base for someone who apparently owned a multi-million euro villa. It did, however, look like the office of a struggling lawyer. Or maybe that was just the impression he wanted to give.

David Perez and Associates, Attorneys- at-Law, said the sign below the frosted glass office door. I was about to knock when I was sure I saw a shadow, through the glass, move away to the left. I hesitated for a couple of seconds, then gave two quick raps.

"Enter," came the abrupt command from a male voice inside.

I opened the door sharply back to the left; it hit something hard and the glass shattered on impact. I ripped the door back and jumped inside. There was a man sitting off to my right behind a large desk, but I hardly had time to notice him. Behind where the door had been was a solidly built dark man, who was crouching low . . . ready to spring at me. He was holding a baseball bat in his right hand, and his left was wiping away some small rivulets of blood from his forehead. Glass injury I guessed.

He swung fast with the bat and caught me across the upper left arm. It hurt like hell! I took a step towards him, and he swung again but missed. In the split-second before he could regain his balance, I stepped in and let him have a hard right to the jaw. That sent him back into the wall. Without waiting for a further invitation, I grabbed his shirt front and smashed him backwards into the wall again. The air flew out of him . . . at both ends. While I still had him by the shirt, I slid him up the wall—he was damn heavy—then ripped him down and drove my knee up into his groin. He grunted hard and doubled over, and I let him drop to the floor. He lay there, clutching his balls, moaning loudly.

I shot a glance quickly across the room, to the pale-faced person behind the desk. "You Perez?" I asked, glaring at him.

"Y–yes," stammered my host.

"Thank you for the charming welcome," I said, and looked down at the gasping figure at my feet, "now what do you suggest I do with this prick—shoot him?"

"Please, no," pleaded Perez, "we didn't know what to expect, so we were just taking precautions."

"Precautions? Waste of fucking time! Look, I didn't come here to physically harm you, but I might change my mind. I want information. I'm conducting a murder investigation, and I believe you can help me. What's the name of this bloke?" I asked, pointing at the still prone figure on the floor.

"Jonas—Jonas Toms, he does some work for me from time to time," said Perez.

"Well Jonas Toms, you get the hell out of here, and leave your bat behind. I might need to use it on your colleague here," I said, as the dark, bruised and cut figure slowly rose.

I looked squarely at Perez. "And you and I will have a chat. Any nonsense and I *will* take the bat to *you*, then have *both of you* charged with assault. Understood?"

Perez nodded agreement nervously, as Jonas Toms, still doubled-over and grasping below his belt buckle, limped quickly out of the office.

CHAPTER TWENTY-EIGHT

D avid Perez was an unremarkable looking man. I guessed in his late-thirties, he was of average height, average build with a small paunch, and a receding hairline. His one redeeming feature was his olive complexion, no doubt due to his Colombian heritage. Dressed in a short-sleeve white shirt, grey trousers and plain, black rubber soled shoes, he looked every inch a perfect fit for the rundown office he occupied. He also looked as if a strong gust of wind would hit him, he might not handle it well.

"Mr Perez," I began, "do you know why I'm here?"

"Yes, n–no," he looked around nervously, his eyes avoiding mine, "I–I'm not sure really."

"Let me fill you in. Three people have been murdered in London. Two of the victims were involved with a Paul Connolly, in business dealings and a previous court case, ten years ago. Names were Andrew Lau and Terry Walker. I was an investigator in that case, and had Connolly jailed for five years as a result."

"What has that got to do with me?"

"In our enquiries this time, we've spoken with Mr Connolly. He lives in a substantial estate in the south of France. He informs us he lives there, rent free, and it is owned by a long-term friend of his, called Dave. He was unable to remember *Dave's* surname. We believe you are that Dave."

"What makes you think that?"

"Our enquiries have also revealed the estate is held in the name of Soacha Capital—a company registered to this very office. You are its sole director and your name is David— so your sign says. Is that correct?"

"Yes, I believe it is correct," he said unconvincingly.

"You *believe* it is correct? Mr Perez, no games—it either is, or is not correct."

"Yes, it is correct."

"Thank you. And tell me, who owns Soacha Capital? Is it you?"

"I'm not at liberty to disclose that," he said abruptly.

Given the jurisdiction we were in, I had to concede that point. "Tell me then, do you know Paul Connolly?"

"I know who he is, but we have never met."

"Then why is it you allow him to live in such a property, controlled by you, rent free?"

"No, no, not rent free. He pays rent . . . six thousand a month."

I rubbed my chin for a moment, to unscramble the thought process. Connolly was apparently broke, and didn't appear to work. Now I was being asked to believe that on top of his enviable lifestyle, he also managed to pay substantial rent.

"So, how does Connolly afford such grandeur?" I asked.

"I have no idea, he just pays the rent." I guessed he was not going to offer to show me receipts.

The whole conversation, I decided, was going nowhere. Perez was stonewalling, hiding behind his very ordinariness. He supposedly knew nothing, and was certainly telling nothing, and there was no legal requirement for him to do so.

Something Marlene Rix had said came back to me—something about a colleague of hers in New York, who knew more about Perez and his earlier life. Maybe I might do better following that line. For a moment I thought of challenging him with the secret information on his sex life, but decided to keep my powder dry. That might be handy, later.

But I couldn't leave the meeting on this note—it was too weak, and he would know he'd beaten me, given me *nothing*. I thought I'd leave him with the impression that I was on to *something*!

"Mr Perez, that will be all *for now*," I said smiling slightly, rising from my chair. His demeanour relaxed noticeably, and he half-smiled in return as he stood. I turned and headed for the door, pulled it open and at the last moment turned back to him. "By the way, our investigations have also revealed *your* involvement with someone else of interest to us. His name is Ernesto Alvarez. Do you know him?"

"Ye–no, I–I'm not sure what you mean," he stammered, stepping backwards. I glared hard at him, and in that moment he suddenly looked so grey and lifeless, I thought *he* might have died.

CHAPTER
TWENTY-NINE

B ack at the hotel I put a call in to Marlene Rix. She was, as usual, very polite and efficient. I told her of my visit to the Perez office, and the reception I'd received from his assistant, Jonas Toms. Assistant or accomplice, I wasn't sure which.

Marlene knew of Jonas Toms—I think she knew of everybody in the Caymans. Small-time crook, but more a standover man. As far as she knew he was the Perez bagman, and if someone couldn't or wouldn't pay, he left them a little physical reminder of the debt they owed.

I told her how unhelpful Perez had been, not that realistically I should have expected anything more. "I think you did well to get him to talk to you at all," she said, "from what I know of him, he is very reclusive. And after his 'outing', even more so."

I expressed my frustration with the case. We had leads, but they always seemed to run dry. My gut feeling was that we were on the right track, but there was still nothing I could pin on anybody. No connection that was obvious, yet.

"You mentioned yesterday a colleague of yours in New York, who knows plenty about Perez. If it's alright with you, I'd like to follow up with him—dig a little deeper into his history. Would you be able to put me in touch with him—I assume it is 'him'?"

"Certainly—I'll give him a call, and if he's okay with it I'll let you know."

I took some time out to inspect the damage left by Jonas Toms and his baseball bat. Nothing broken, but man it had left a mighty bruise. I found some cream in my travelling medical kit, and gently rubbed it into the red, raised welt on my left shoulder. That hurt!

Ten minutes later the phone rang. Marlene Rix had contacted her friend, who was only too happy to help another officer in the line of duty. I took down the name and number, and thanked her profusely. Where had *she* been ten years ago? I could have used her on the Connolly case then. In fact, she'd be great to have on my team now.

I dialled the number, and a distinct Bronx accent answered—"Lanfranchi here."

"Lieutenant Commander Dan Lanfranchi?" I asked.

"Yes sir, what can I do for you?"

"Ash Todd from the Australian Federal Police here—I believe Marlene Rix has spoken to you about me?"

"Yes sir, she mentioned you are in the Caymans and might need some help regarding a Mr David Perez down there."

"That's correct," I said, "I understand he is originally from New Jersey and New York, and Marlene tells me that you have a detailed knowledge of him."

"I know a bit about him. If you're interested in basic detail of Perez only, I can do that in an e-mail to Marlene for you. But I assume you might want more on him *and* his colleagues. If that's the case, I would not put it in writing—I'd want you here. That way I can give you a proper understanding of what you're dealing with."

"Thanks Lieutenant, I think a visit would be a smart move. You available tomorrow?"

"Afternoon's fine—say two o'clock?"

"See you at two."

Now we might get somewhere. Let's dig a little deeper behind the Perez facade, and see what that brings us. I could hardly wait to get on the plane, but first I needed to let McClure know my movements and fill him in on my meeting with Perez.

He was out of the office. Cindy, however, was in and we had a long chat. I gave her a quick rundown on Perez and told her of my upcoming meeting with Lanfranchi in New York. I was missing her already, and it had only been a couple of days.

"I'll let the DCI know, but don't be too long Ash . . . it's getting lonely here."

That beautiful, velvet voice had me hungering to get back to London.

CHAPTER THIRTY

I grabbed a morning American Airlines flight into LaGuardia, then a cab to the Hotel Mulberry in Manhattan. After I checked in, it was only a short walk from there to NYPD headquarters at 1 Police Plaza.

I arrived at Lanfranchi's office on the eighth floor a little before two, but he was ready and waiting for me. We shook hands as he ushered me inside.

"Welcome Commander," he said warmly, "coffee?"

"Yes thanks, and forget the formality—call me Ash—and thank you for agreeing to see me at such short notice."

"No problem at all, anything I can do to help nail bad dudes—only too happy. And while we're on first name terms, call me Franch—everyone else does so you might as well be on the same page. Now, what do you want to know?"

I explained my involvement with Scotland Yard and their murder investigation; the connection to Connolly from ten years prior; and a discovery of the link, however loose at this stage, with Perez.

"Trouble is Franch, I can't seem to get a provable connection between any of them. Connolly and Perez are damn nervous ... like first-time expectant fathers, and both act as dumb as the latest blonde joke. Whatever their *real* relationship, they're not talking, and without some firm evidence I can't force them to. I can maybe scare them a bit, but that's it."

"Sounds like you need the entire NYPD as backup," Lanfranchi laughed, "but seriously, I have some lowdown on Perez. Maybe not enough to get him to talk, but I've got a few ideas in that area."

Lanfranchi went on to explain how he headed a detective unit in the Organised Crime Control Bureau. Prior to that he'd spent eighteen years in the force, working under-cover for about four of them before getting out with his life intact ... just. His patch covered every aspect of major criminal outfits from narcotics, extortion and gun-running, to murder. I sipped my coffee and listened intently.

"That's quite a CV," I said after he had finished, "makes mine look like a B-grader. But what about Perez . . . is he a graduate from *those schools*?"

"Nah . . . not the balls for any of that. He's part of a big Colombian community in Union City, New Jersey. The Colombians are well entrenched in that part of town—they conduct many legitimate businesses, but they also conduct their share of corrupt ones. And they stick together like glue."

"Is there a way in to their network?" I asked.

"There is, but it won't be for publication. I did undercover work in that area for a few years, a sort of swap arrangement between the NYPD and the New Jersey force. There are two or three people I'd trust; people I could talk to, and know it would go no further. That said, there are probably two or three hundred people I would not want to talk to, no matter what. That should give you some idea of what we're up against."

"Is there anything I can do to start the ball rolling—to be of help somehow?"

"Not for now. Just be back here tomorrow morning at ten. We'll go over to Union City and meet one of those two or three people I mentioned. And dress so you don't look like a cop—like you're on holiday is good."

I stood and thanked him again. "See you in the morning," I said as I turned towards the office door.

"As I said," Lanfranchi said almost as an afterthought, "these people stick together like glue. They also stick with what works for them. They have a big retail presence in New Jersey—maybe that might help you as a place to start in London. By the way, does anyone else know you are here?"

"No—not really. Marlene Rix and Roberts in the Caymans of course, and McClure in London. Plus maybe four or five more in Scotland Yard," I said, thinking harder. "Why do you ask?"

"No real reason," said Lanfranchi, as he stared out over the parkland below, "but these people always seem able to know your every move, even if you've never had any dealing with them before. What's more, the source of their information will be the person you are *least likely* to think of. See you tomorrow."

Now he really did have me thinking hard!

CHAPTER
THIRTY-ONE

E rnesto Alvarez sat on the terrace of his apartment high above Park Lane in Mayfair, sipping his aguapanela and gazing across the rooftops of London to The Eye. The wealthiest of this great city are all below me, he thought. This is good.

What was not so good, was his loneliness. Now nearing seventy, he had lived a solitary existence for a few years, and every day was spent solo in this big, empty house. Not that he didn't appreciate it—after all he *had* paid £14 million five years earlier—it's just that he had no one else to share it with.

Then again, his life was not one of shar-ing. Sure he had his driver, who was also his butler, but he was an employee—not someone he envisaged spending his life with. The security system—installed at a cost of half a million—meant no-one else could get in. Enforced isolation was necessary. Even his children, now fully grown and part of the business, could not casually drop by.

Nor was he free to simply step outside for a walk. He was surrounded by parks—some of the most beautiful and famous in Britain—but they were off-limits. Ah, the price of success. Or more correctly, the price of success in *his* line of business.

Yes, he mused, *his business.* He thought back more than sixty years, to the backstreets of Bogota. The smell, the sweat, the dirt—all so long ago, and left a long way behind. And then, as a young boy growing up in Union City, New Jersey. His family moved there after World War II, renting a small apartment on 41st Street, his father finding work across the Hudson in the meatpacking district.

At fifteen he left school and started work for the Gamez brothers. School held little interest for him—the lure of business was what kept him awake at night—and he spent his spare time hanging around the Gamez warehouse, hoping they might give him some task ... anything to get a start. They were major players in the import-export world— migrants from Cuba in the 1950s, who imported, amongst other things, cigars. They controlled the trade, and they obviously saw a spark in the young Alvarez, because he was soon their youngest deliveryman.

He learnt the business quickly, particularly the very profitable parts. Cigarettes, under the counter stuff of course, and stolen cars were both big contributors to the Gamez empire. With huge numbers of Cubans migrating to the US in the 1960s, Gamez Brothers were in the middle of an exploding market. And it was virtually *all cash*.

The young Alvarez couldn't sit still though—his Colombian roots burned strongly. The marijuana trade had begun to boom, and he was just the man to get it out onto the streets of New York. He had the connections, both from his time with Gamez and his family in South America. He was on his way.

Trouble was ... America was a competitive market. Everybody wanted a piece of the action—cops, politicians, not to mention those who fancied themselves as vital parts of the syndicate. Everyone was on the up—even if they did nothing.

Just like Joe Garcia.

Garcia was a petty criminal who mostly knocked off cars. But he was older than Alvarez, and thought he could run things, his way. He wanted a slice of every sale, and his contribution? Nothing, except the odd threat of violence if Alvarez refused to pay.

Eventually, like all lazy quitters, he took the threat too far. Garcia called Rodriguez, the Alvarez supplier in Columbia, and offered to do the same work as Alvarez but for a smaller cut.

Alvarez had made all the connections, ensured all the supply lines through New York ran smoothly, and now this turkey wanted to claim it for himself. There was only one way to deal with him. A 9:00 p.m. meeting on Little West 12th Street, not far from where Alvarez Sr had worked for all those years in meat-packing, and a single shot to the head stopped Garcia and his crap for good.

The heat from the shooting, particularly from Garcia's family and associates, became too heavy. Plus there was a new drug of choice for the discerning, white user—

cocaine. Alvarez decided that greener pastures lay elsewhere. To escape the Garcia fallout, he took a trip to France, and then to London. He had landed in *paradise*.

London in the sixties was trendy and hot... swinging. Plus, the Brits had a more genteel approach to business—less in-your-face. Alvarez knew an opportunity when he saw one, and this one screamed at him in *capitals*. Six months later, armed with stamped immigration papers and the blessing of Rodriguez in Bogota, Ernesto Alvarez was the new face of the cartel in the United Kingdom. Same formula... Rodriguez supplied, Alvarez distributed. Bingo!

Almost forty years on, and he had been the undisputed king of narcotic importation for most of that time. Here he was, high above the London skyline, looking over his client base and he should have been pleased. Now, however, he had a new threat to deal with. It was not serious, *yet*, but like all threats he had learned to deal with them early, and convincingly.

This policeman from Australia, Commander Ashley Todd, had the potential to cause great harm. He was not on the payroll. Enquiries had revealed he was incorruptible—and this, for someone in Alvarez position, was *not* a useful trait. Therefore, his momentum should be terminated as soon as possible.

Yes, decided Ernesto Alvarez, it was time to put a call into New York.

CHAPTER
THIRTY-TWO

I t was ten-fifteen on a hot, humid New York morning, when Lieutenant Commander Lanfranchi and I exited police headquarters in his unmarked, dark blue, Chevrolet Impala. "We're going to see Tommy, an old friend from my undercover days; we keep in touch," said Lanfranchi. It was a little after eleven when we pulled up on Bergenline Avenue in Union City, just over the Hudson.

We walked about thirty paces and turned left into a side street for about another thirty, then left again into a small laneway which gave access to the rear of the neighbourhood shops. The area consisted of a variety of unremarkable one and two storey buildings, mostly restaurants of undeterminable quality, an accountancy firm, laundromat, supermarket, and a bar.

We entered the rear of the building housing the bar, which covered the entire site from Bergenline through to the laneway. Lanfranchi knocked sharply on the door and called out, "you in Tommy?"

A crackly Latin American voice called back from a room just inside the rear door, "that you Franch?"

"One and the same," said Lanfranchi as we stepped inside, and around boxes of liquor and cigarettes.

We entered a small room... a dimly-lit, yellowish colour and maybe fifteen feet by fifteen, square. Cigarette smoke haze hung at head-height. I coughed a couple of times. There was worn linoleum on the floor, one high-up window partly open, two faded, brown-cloth armchairs, and a timber desk piled high with papers and more cigarette boxes. Behind the desk sat a diminutive man in a white shirt, completely bald and I guessed he must have been at least eighty. He stood as we entered the room, and held out his hand to Lanfranchi.

"You keeping well Tommy?" asked Lanfranchi.

"Good as can be expected under the circumstances," said the small man, smiling through nicotine stained teeth. "Business is tough, though."

"I bet it is," said Lanfranchi, turning to me and winking, "you must be down to your last thirty or forty apartments by now." The small man waved Lanfranchi's comment away with the back of his hand. "Tommy, I want you to meet Commander Ashley Todd from the Australian Federal Police. Ash . . . meet Tommy."

I held out my hand to shake his, as he stiffly peered up at me. He only seemed to come up slightly above my navel, and my hand was about twice the size of his, but he still had a firm grip. "Thank you for agreeing to see me," I said.

"What can I do for you Commander?" wheezed Tommy, offering me a cigarette which I declined.

"Ash—call me Ash. I'm investigating a triple murder in London—assisting Scotland Yard—and my enquiries have led me to the door of a certain David Perez," I explained. "I haven't yet made the connection with Perez,

but Lieutenant Commander Lanfranchi, sorry ...
Franch ... has brought me to you. I guess he
thought you might know something about
him."

Tommy glanced at Lanfranchi, who looked
directly at him and nodded slowly once or
twice. I took this to be a signal that I could be
trusted.

"I know him," said Tommy, "but I haven't
seen him for a long time. He grew up here and
went to school here. I knew his parents well—
good people. Father was in the car business,
used to sell autos."

"What about his work," I asked, "do you
know what he did after school?"

"Law school," continued Tommy, "at Rutgers,
then he went to work for a local law firm called
Rojas and Dias. They had an office a few
blocks further down on Bergenline. I thought
he might become a partner there, take over
from them because they were fairly old, but
he left maybe ten or more years ago."

"And then?"

Tommy seemed to stiffen noticeably,
drew in a long breath and let it out very
slowly. He stared at the papers on his desk;
the silence lasted for probably a full minute.

Just like at a military commemoration, or a funeral, a minute's silence seems to last half an hour. He glanced at Lanfranchi, who nodded again.

"Moved to a religious group in New York City. On 60th Street I think. Outfit called Calima Ministries. He was their legal man, but if you ask me, they were no religious group. All bullshit—just a front," said Tommy.

"What makes you say that—why do you think they are a front?" I asked.

"Were; not are. A few years later I heard Perez had left, and this Calima had closed. Don't know where he went, or what happened to him. But it's the asshole behind Calima that made me think it was a front. He and religion are polar opposites. The only thing *they* have in common, is that both are used for starting wars."

"And who is this person behind Calima, this *asshole*?"

Tommy's dark eyes narrowed, and for the first time he glared straight at me. I know the look of hatred when I see it, and Tommy's old, brown, lined face was full of it.

"This fucking asshole's name," Tommy spat, "is *Ernesto Alvarez*."

CHAPTER
THIRTY-THREE

Oscar Jesus Garcia, known through-out New Jersey as Tommy, was a very successful man. Born just on eighty years ago, Tommy had lived his entire working life in and around Union City. Like so many Latin American families, Tommy's had moved to the US following World War II.

Life for the migrant families was tough. While there was plenty of work after the war, a father with limited English and skills could only attract a menial, physically demanding job. The prospect of owning your home was just a dream for most, but families were happy for the opportunity to at least get work, and a chance to create a future with hope for their children.

And so it was for the Garcia family. Garcia Senior worked as a motor mechanic.

They rented a modest, two-bedroom apartment, with Tommy and his three brothers crammed into the tiny second bedroom. Their parents wanted them to go to university, but financially that was never going to happen. The boys, for their part, all just wanted to finish school sooner rather than later.

Despite having formal Colombian names, the boys were given Anglicised nicknames; something that would fit right in with Middle America. Bobby and Michael were the two oldest, and as each reached the age of sixteen they left school, and New Jersey, forever. Bobby, like his father, was keen on automobiles. He headed straight for Detroit, got a job with General Motors, and never left either. He died, too young, in his late-fifties.

Michael was keen on surfing, not that much was available in Union City. He'd seen enough on television, however, and left home working odd-jobs across the country. As soon as he could afford it, he headed for Hawaii. He opened a chain of surf shops, and now in his mid-eighties he enjoyed a comfortable life in his own nirvana.

That just left the twins—Tommy and Joe. Tommy was only small, but he was a livewire. He loved people and life. He got a job with a firm of liquor distributors; not the legal variety as he was too young, but he didn't know any better. They didn't ask questions about his age, so the issue never arose.

To him they were a respectable, normal company. He got on with their customers, his sales took off, and they paid him well. By the time he reached legal drinking age, he'd been working for nearly five years and was well into paying off his first apartment. He'd saved a chunk for a deposit, and his employer financed the rest.

Tommy then made two major decisions about his own life. The first was that he would work for himself, preferably in the liquor industry as that was what he knew and loved. The second was that he would buy his mother and father their own place, as soon as he could, so they could enjoy it before they got too old.

It took him just two years . . . both of these he achieved by the age of twenty-three. He had paid off his own apartment, and his next big commission check went straight to the purchase of a home for his parents. Again the balance was financed by his employer. He then set about establishing his own liquor retailing operation.

His employer didn't want to lose him, and he needed their finance, so they struck a deal. Tommy wanted to establish a legitimate bar, but with some extra grunt— a small, low-key gambling outlet at the rear. This, of course, was not so legitimate, but could be very profitable.

His employer's business had grown so much, they'd had been forced to become more mainstream, and had established a large general-liquor wholesaling division. This department would supply Tommy's bar, they would finance the setup, and Tommy would continue to look after their biggest ten or twelve original customers. Everyone was happy—and to help keep everything running smoothly, Tommy put brother Joe in to manage the bar.

Despite being twins, Tommy and Joe were totally different. Joe was big and strong. He didn't like work, and had little ambition except to make as much as he could, by doing as little as possible. He fell in with a rough crowd ... edgy young guys who spent a lot of time hanging around street corners, smoking, doing not much ... and resorted to dumb stuff like knocking off cars for the re-birthing racket.

Blood, as they say, runs thicker than water, and despite Joe's ordinary attempts at commercial life, Tommy loved him. He knew he would have to watch Joe like a hawk, that with all the cash and grog at his disposal Joe might be severely tempted, but it was worth the punt. For the next five or six years, it worked like magic.

Joe, for the most part, kept his hands out of the till, and stayed mostly sober. Tommy's businesses raked in the moolah. He established more bars, more gambling dens, each financed by his original employer, and he paid them off quickly, in cash. He bought more properties, including one for Joe, and sent his parents on a round-the-world trip.

Then trouble arrived in the form of drugs. Politicians got involved and started a *'war'* on them. Their phoney *'war'*, just like Prohibition before it, presented massive opportunities for people like Tommy, who had the right connections. He was approached to distribute through his outlets, but declined. There was always a physical risk in saying no to the drug cartels, but Tommy was determined to resist as long as possible.

Joe, however, could not say no, and he started dealing on the side. Minor stuff at first, mostly marijuana, none of which caused any great distress. Then came cocaine—everyone wanted it and the money to be made was huge. Joe could see dollar signs, *mega dollars*, for virtually no work. One thing lay in his way—the supply into New York, and therefore New Jersey, was controlled by one man— Ernesto Alvarez.

Joe, the fool, decided to go direct to the supply source in Colombia ... cut Alvarez out. You try to circumvent a successful operator at your own peril, particularly someone like Alvarez. A ruthless native of New Jersey, he had gold-plated contacts, super-efficient distribution lines, and absolutely no conscience. Every action was taken to ensure the advancement of his business, and nothing was allowed to interfere.

Alvarez got rid of Joe in the time honoured gangster tradition ... a single shot to the head. Straight from the mob handbook. Tommy found the pain of losing his twin more unbearable than he could have imagined. He had always run his business on the basis of not harbouring grudges, even though his industry gave him plenty of opportunity to do just that. But Tommy figured life had to go on, each person was charting their own course, and the universe had a knack for restoring the balance.

For a short period he engaged some of his own contacts to hunt Alvarez for revenge, but then decided to ignore him instead, and let the universe do its thing. Alvarez disappeared from his world. Now, forty years on, Alvarez' name was reappearing. Even now, after all this time, Tommy felt the tide of anger and disgust rise within him. Maybe now the universe was ready. And maybe this thumping-big commander from Australia was just the man to carry it out.

CHAPTER
THIRTY-FOUR

L anfranchi dropped me back at the Hotel Mulberry after our visit to Tommy Garcia in Union City. Franch gave me a rundown on Tommy's history, on how Tommy had the best connections on the Street, and how those connections had saved Franch's life on more than one occasion when he was working undercover. To repay the debt, Franch had supplied Tommy with tip-offs on raids by the gaming squad, and any underground movement from potential competitors. Despite the age difference, and the fact Franch was now 'big-time in head office', they were best buddies.

I grabbed a bite to eat at the coffee shop in the hotel, then went to my room to put a call in to McClure. Cindy came on the line, explaining McClure was at a meeting and would be returning shortly. I marvelled again at that smooth, sweet voice, which again had me longing for her to be in my arms. I collected my thoughts, gave her a quick run-through on my meeting with Lanfranchi and Tommy, and asked her to get McClure to give me a ring.

Fifteen minutes later the hotel phone buzzed with McClure on the other end. "How are you keeping Ash—you okay?" he asked.

"Fine Jim, and you?"

"We're all good here, but we've hit a dead-end with any further evidence on our murders. You got anything more?"

I went over my meeting in Union City, and that my gut feeling was that we were getting closer to the nerve centre. I now had two vital bits of information on David Perez; not that they were sufficient to have him convicted of anything, but they might allow me to put more pressure on him. It would mean another trip back to the Caymans though. But first, I wanted to follow up with Tommy Garcia. I felt sure there was more to what he knew, but it might take another visit, or two, for him to trust me enough to open up.

McClure agreed. "Stay safe Ash. You know my thoughts on this territory you're getting into. Let me know if you need anything from me."

"Thanks mate—I'll let you know. I'll see how the rest of today pans out, see what else I can find... I'll call about the same time tomorrow."

I decided to stay in the hotel room for a bit, mull over my next move, and maybe catch a few zeds. The complimentary USA Today looked a good place to begin.

I woke with a start. My room phone was buzzing again, and I was confused. Where was I? It took a few moments to regain my bearings, and I picked up the phone expecting McClure or Lanfranchi to be on the end. A slightly muffled voice came on... "is that Commander Todd?"

"Yes, who is this?"

"My name is Tony Lopez and I work for Tommy. He would like you to come and meet with him again. You available now?"

I hadn't met anyone called Tony, however I was keen to hear anything Tommy might have for me. At least he was chasing me, which was better than the other way round. "Sure, what time and where do I go?"

"Different place than before. There's another bar, further along Bergenline near 35th Street, has a rear entrance. Same deal—come round the back—no later than seven." The phone went dead.

I glanced at the hotel clock. I must have fallen asleep for hours, as it was now five-thirty. No time to waste—it was evening peak and I guessed it would take at least an hour to get there, maybe more. I made a quick visit to the bathroom, grabbed my coat, and bolted for the lobby to nail a cab.

CHAPTER THIRTY-FIVE

J ust as I thought, it took about an hour and twenty to reach the area around Bergenline and 35th. The first twenty minutes was spent just finding a taxi, the rest sitting in bumper-to-bumper traffic. I had the driver drop me a couple of blocks away so I could walk and take in the area. A little bit of reconnaissance for no real reason—just force of habit. A low-key arrival seemed sensible.

The neighbourhood looked much like the one earlier where I met Tommy, but I couldn't see any bar which looked similar. I crossed over 35th Street and spotted a liquor store on the opposite side of Bergenline and a little further down. I assumed that must be the place, so I walked past it and turned into a side street. Again there was a small lane which appeared to lead back behind the store, but it was now dark so I slowed my pace and kept close to the wall of the neighbouring building.

There was a gate, slightly open into a small courtyard, and about eight or ten paces inside a dim light lit the rear door. I approached it slowly, and about halfway across the courtyard my phone rang. I grabbed it and answered impatiently, "yes?"

It was Lanfranchi. "Hey Ash—happy with our meeting earlier today?" he asked breezily.

"Great," I whispered loudly, "but I can't talk much now. One of Tommy's men rang . . . said Tommy wanted to meet with me, so I'm just about there."

"Who rang you?"

"Tony—Tony Lopez. He works for Tommy."

Lanfranchi sounded impatient. "Where are you, where are you meeting him?" he demanded.

"At one of his other stores, further down Bergenline, past 35th . . ."

"Damn it, Ash . . . get the . . ."

At that moment I heard a slight shuffle behind me; I half-turned to see what it was, and *everything went black.*

CHAPTER THIRTY-SIX

This was wrong! I was lying on a cold floor and it was dark except for a thin sliver of light showing under a door. The back of my head hurt... the pain ran down my neck, across my shoulder. This, I was sure, was not where I was meant to be, but I couldn't for the life of me think where I *was* meant to be.

I looked to my left, but could only make out a wall about six feet away, and nothing else. I rolled partly on to my right side, and could make out some boxes stacked high, and a plain, metal chair partially highlighted by the door light.

I sat up slowly. My hands were free, which was something, but my ankles were bound in what appeared to be steel hobbles, connected by a chain. I couldn't see them very well, but from the feel I guessed they were what might have been used on convicts, or a prison gang. Either way, I wasn't going to move anywhere too fast in them. But where was I?

I tried to think and slowly the events came back to me. Lanfranchi's call was the last I could remember. I listened for sounds— maybe there was someone talking, but it was muffled and not close, so I couldn't make anything of it. I clambered onto my knees, then crawled to the chair and sat on it. It was only small, and with my frame I seemed to overlap it everywhere, but at least it was more comfortable than the floor.

I had to think what to do. Number one problem were the shackles and number two, I had no idea where I was. Maybe I was in the back of the liquor store, where I'd come to meet Tommy. But this didn't seem like Tommy's doing, and if it wasn't him, who in the hell was it? If I could shuffle to the door, and by some miracle found it unlocked, I still faced the daunting task of shuffling to free-dom. I'd be picked off in a heartbeat, and God knows what was on the other side of that door.

I was still trying to clear my head and decide what to do when I heard voices getting closer. What sounded like two, or maybe three, men stopped outside the door, and they were obviously discussing me. I could hear one say "let's see if the bastard's come to." The door flew open tossing a shaft of light straight onto me perched on the tiny chair.

Two men stepped inside and threw on the light, which temporarily blinded me after my time in the dark. I was sure there was a third, but he didn't appear in the room. I put my hands over my eyes, but one of the men produced a pistol and pushed it straight into my temple. "Hands down or die!" he demanded.

I slowly dropped my hands and at the same time, dropped my head, so as to get some focus back. The other began walking around me, circling like a bird of prey. Neither spoke for probably a minute.

"What are you doing here?" the other finally asked, in a slight Latino accent. I squinted up at him. He seemed about forty, fairly thin and a little over six feet, with a mop of oily, black hair and a pockmarked face.

"I came to meet Tommy. Are you Tony Lopez?"

"Stuff Tommy," said the first, a shorter, fat man about the same age. I noted his stomach was so large, the bottom two buttons on his shirt had popped. He produced the pistol again, and pushed it up under my chin this time. "And no fucking questions. Now, what are you doing in New York, and in New Jersey?"

I had to think quickly. These two apparently had nothing to do with Tommy, and I had no idea who they belonged to, but it obviously wasn't good. I reverted to basic police training... interrogation procedure straight from the manual. "My name is Todd and I am a commander with the Australian Federal Police. My police number is 266..."

"We know *who* you are," said the thin one, "it's *what* you are doing here we want to know. Now, in order to avoid upsetting my colleague, tell me *why you are here!*" he yelled, thumping his fist into the boxes.

"As I said, I am a commander with the Australian Federal police and I am here as part of an exchange training program with the NYPD..."

"*Bullshit*," screamed the thin one, and spun round to face his colleague. "Go and get Tony and tell him to bring the hand machine. Now!"

The short, fat one gave a big sigh and waddled out. Thin stood and glared at me for a few moments. "Let's see if this helps improve your memory," he sneered, as the fat one and another—I guessed the one I thought I'd heard earlier—entered the room.

The new recruit, Tony, said nothing and moved directly to my right side. He was holding a small, metal object which had a top and bottom flat surface, and a large handle shaped like a key. The fat man stood by my left side, produced his pistol and pushed it under my chin again. The thin one stood in front, bent forward so his face was level with mine, and through stained teeth and a nicotine stink that took my breath away, growled "give him a *hand*, Tony."

Tony slipped the machine across my right fingers, and sharply turned the key. It must have had some ratchet type mechanism, because with a couple of quick turns the pain was unbearable. I gritted my teeth.

"Try again," sneered the thin one, "now, what are you doing here?"

"Training exchange . . ." I spluttered, barely able to open my mouth, "with the . . ."

"Tony!" snapped the thin one, and the machine tightened another notch. I let out a guttural grunt.

"This time!" demanded the thin one again.

"NYPD," I gasped, "train . . ."

"Tony!" yelled the thin one, and the machine ratcheted again. I felt something snap in my fingers and let out a roar.

The fat one jumped back and fired his gun at the ceiling. "Shut the fuck up, or I give the next one to you!" he screamed.

The thin one turned quickly and smacked the fat one across the back of the head. "Idiot, no shooting yet. Not until I say so. Put the gun under his head." The fat one did as he was told, and sweating profusely, jammed the pistol back under my chin. The pain in my hand was intense, burning . . . I thought I'd black out.

"For the last time Mr Commander Todd," said the thin one, resuming his position in front, "if you give us any more crap, we will break all your fingers, then shoot you. Now..."

I had to think of *something*. "Okay, okay," I said, again through gritted teeth, "I am here looking for someone."

"That's better. Who are you looking for?"

What the hell, I thought, they're a pack of apprentice gangsters, but they just might kill me. Time for a punt. "I'm looking for Ern..."

I had no chance to finish. The door smashed open, and in jumped Lanfranchi and a second man I'd never seen before. Both the thin and fat ones turned towards them at the moment the commotion started. Lanfranchi took two steps and let rip a left hook into the fat one's head, which sent him smashing into the wall, and the pistol backwards into the boxes. Franch's colleague, who must have been nearly as big as me, grabbed the thin one with both hands, picked him up and threw him over my head into the boxes behind.

Tony, who still had hold of the machine with my hand in it, appeared paralysed by fear, gaping open-mouthed at the action. I stood up, towering over him by about a foot and growled, "Take that OFF!" He stared blankly up at me, but registered nothing.

Terror, I guess. I ripped my left hand straight up, and smashed his lower jaw. He coughed once, producing a tooth and a drool of blood from the corner of his mouth. He hit the floor, out cold.

"You okay?" asked Lanfranchi.

"Just dandy, but get this thing off me," I said, shoving the torture device in his face. "And I can't walk."

Lanfranchi looked at my feet and laughed, then turned to his colleague. "Bob, meet Commander Todd. Get that vice off his hand, will you?" I nodded at Bob thankfully, who quickly removed it.

Lanfranchi turned and gingerly lifted my right-hand. "Hmm—I think we'd better get someone to look at that—make sure nothing is broken."

He moved over to the thin one, grabbed his shirt front and reefed him upward. "Where's the key to the leg irons, asshole?" He pointed weakly towards the fat one, who remained unconscious.

"Bob, search that turkey for the key and remove them. We can't have a visiting commander hopping from a crime scene, can we?" Lanfranchi said, laughing.

Bob found the key and undid my shackles. "Right, gentlemen," said Lanfranchi, "I think we're ready to leave." He surveyed the crushed boxes and prostrate bodies, then stooped to pick up the pistol which earlier had been in the possession of the fat one.

Lanfranchi stepped over to the thin one again, bent down and shoved the barrel hard up under his chin. His eyes opened wide as a look of sheer panic gripped him. Lanfranchi looked right through his face. "Tell your boss Tommy sends his regards."

Then as Lanfranchi slowly took the gun away, and the thin one momentarily relaxed, he let rip with a right to his jaw. The crunch and snap at impact even made me grimace. I don't think thin would remember.

CHAPTER THIRTY-SEVEN

L anfranchi took me to the New York Downtown Hospital, which was right near his office and not too far from my hotel. Apparently they knew a lot of the NYPD detectives there, and Franch was able to sneak me through ahead of the queue of usual nightly traumas. They took x-rays of my hand, and although it was badly bruised there was no break. I offered for him to leave me, to save him the wait, saying I could walk home. He declined, saying "no way buddy, I nearly lost you once tonight and I'm not going to risk it again."

On the ride to the hospital Franch explained what had happened to me, apart from the obvious that is. After his call to me went dead, he had rung Tommy who knew nothing of the meeting. He also knew no Tony Lopez.

Franch told him where the meeting was meant to be, behind the liquor store, and how the call had ended. Tommy said "shit Franch, that shop is just a front. You gotta go get him out of there."

"So I grabbed Bob . . . he's one of my team and has worked undercover with me before, so he knows the ropes. Luckily we got to you before they did too much damage," said Lanfranchi.

After the hospital had finished with me, we took Franch's car back to the hotel. He put a call in to Tommy to update him with the night's activities. Tommy came on the speakerphone. "You did well . . . like I said before, that place has always been a front, mostly drugs. I heard there's some Tony associated with it, but I don't know him, or his real name."

"Well," said Franch, "they were definitely after our big friend here, and they meant to do him harm."

"True," I cut in, "but I don't think they were going to kill me, despite their threats."

"That's the strange bit," said Tommy, "because I reckon you were odds-on to be sliced and diced by now."

"Why do you say that?" asked Lanfranchi.

"Because it's how they operate," said Tommy, continuing with some bitterness in his voice. "You see, for at least thirty years the drug operation at that shop has been supplied and controlled, by friends, if you can call them that, *of your man Alvarez.*"

CHAPTER
THIRTY-EIGHT

It was approaching midnight when I finally got back to my hotel room, nursing my bandaged right hand, and a packet of painkillers provided by the hospital. Thankfully, the rest of me was intact right down to my Glock, which Bob had remembered to collect from the torture room as we left. The way things were heading, I'd be needing it.

I began to work out my next move. I was exhausted, but felt too tired to go to sleep. Sort of jittery, I guess. I poured myself a double whiskey from the hotel mini-bar and settled on the sofa, when the thought of Sally suddenly sprang into my mind. She had completely disappeared from my world for days. I called our home number—it was the middle of the day back in Sydney, and I knew she would be at work—but at least I could leave a message.

I did just that. It was a long message given all I had just been through, but I wanted to at least make it sound as though I was interested enough in her ... in *us* ... and I assumed she would be too. The strange thing was when I came to sign off with my usual "I love you" I faltered, just for a second, before saying it. It made me feel uneasy, because at that moment I realised as far as *we* were concerned, I really doubted that I was 'in love'. *Confused,* more likely.

Sleep was what I desperately needed. I grabbed a couple of the room magazines, and crawled into bed. That, and the whiskey, had the desired effect ... I was out like a light before I'd finished the first page.

I awoke to another hot and humid New York morning, showered, and took a long walk around Manhattan, mingling with the early-morning commuters. It was such a noisy, frantic, busy city ... made Sydney seem like a country town. But it seemed to give a constant charge of adrenaline, which was intoxicating and somewhat addictive. I could see why people either loved or hated the place—I hadn't thought about it much before, but in my case it was definitely the former.

I found a small bakery, and settled in for breakfast. My hand didn't hurt nearly as much as I'd expected; maybe it was the painkillers, but either way once I'd finished the biggest feed I'd had in a long while, I felt really good, on top of the world. My phone rang with Lanfranchi on the other end.

"How's the hand?" he asked.

"Nearly like new, but I hope I don't have to use it on anyone," I laughed. "And thanks for last night—I'd have been in deep shit without you."

"No problem Ash, *'protect and serve'* is our job here. But do me a favour . . . don't go talking to people without checking with me first. I don't want to be a nursemaid to you, but it might keep both of us alive a bit longer if I know in advance who you're going into battle with."

"Okay, okay I got the message. So, what excitement do you have planned for me today?" I asked, with just a hint of sarcasm.

"As a matter of fact I do have something for you. Tommy rang me earlier, concerned about you after last night. I told him not to worry; that you were too big and strong for three of those jerks. But he has more info which he thinks might be useful, so he wants to meet with you again. If you can get yourself to his office where we met yesterday, at three this afternoon, I'll see you there."

I knew it! I knew Tommy had not told me everything at our first meeting. This is what I was after, and all six feet five inches, and two hundred and seventy-five pounds of me, bounced out the bakery and into the New York heat.

CHAPTER
THIRTY-NINE

I arrived at Tommy's office, around the back as before, at three o'clock as Lanfranchi had requested. I knocked on the door and Franch's familiar voice called out for me to join them. I entered the smoke-filled room, where two other men I had never seen before were seated around Tommy's desk, between him and Lanfranchi. Franch and Tommy stood and greeted me, but the other two remained sitting and fixed me with a steady gaze.

"Ash, these are friends of Tommy—Dom and Manny—and this is Commander Todd," said Lanfranchi addressing the seated pair, "so, over to you Tommy." Each nodded to me, but made no effort to rise. I merely nodded back.

Tommy explained that Dom had a background in finance, and was from Manhattan. He certainly looked the part; tallish I assumed, as he was still chair-bound, thin build and well-dressed with a good-looking, olive complexion and greying, wavy hair. I guessed he was a well preserved sixty-year-old or thereabouts, and probably of Italian background.

Manny was younger, maybe forty-five... short and dark with a stocky muscular build. He looked as I imagined Tommy must have looked, at about the same age.

"Manny is from the street—from the same industry as me, only he works on the wholesale side. That, and information," said Tommy. "I'd trust these two with my life."

I nodded, showing my understanding of the relationship. I looked across at Lanfranchi, who was listening casually but otherwise unmoved.

"Word is," continued Tommy, "that the goons who roughed you up yesterday got their order from the top. Isn't that right Manny?"

"That's what I heard," said Manny, speaking for the first time. "Strange thing is though; they obviously had orders not to kill you. Those at the top never get involved if it's just a warning—they only come in if they want someone terminated. So if they have given the order, but want you spared, you must have some respect going on up there."

"I have *no* idea," I replied, "I don't know who I'm dealing with. I've never seen them before in my life."

"Like I told you," cut in Tommy, "the top of that tree is Alvarez. My bet is he gave the order."

We all sat in silence for a few moments, letting the idea that Alvarez was now controlling my fate, sink in.

"One thing to keep in mind, something that might help," said Manny as an afterthought, "whoever you're after, if you go chasing these people, just remember they like retail outlets as a front—just like their liquor shop."

"But that's not all I wanted you here for," said Tommy, "you were asking about David Perez?" I nodded. "Tell him Dom."

Dom sat up taller in his chair, then lent forward with elbows on knees, and rested his chin on his clasped hands.

"I believe you know that Perez was a lawyer here in Union City, then moved across to New York City to run a show called Calima Ministries?" asked Dom.

"Yes, Tommy has filled me in on that part."

Dom explained that he had started out as a stock broker, and then moved into investment banking twenty years ago. He gained an intimate knowledge of the liquor and gaming industries during that time, which is how he'd got to know Tommy.

Seven or eight years ago, having made his pile, he left investment banking and established his own financial advocacy. "Left the corporate world behind, but I still wanted something to do so as not to get bored. So now I work with real people ... y'know, the ones who financially get belted up by life, and the system ... see if I can help them. And Tommy sends me plenty of *real* people who need *real* help."

"I see," I said, "but what is your connection with Perez and Calima?"

"Back, a few years before I left investment banking, Calima Ministries came on the scene. It was strange, because at first blush you would expect them to be a religious organisation judging by the name. That's what we thought they were, sort of a charitable group ... you know ... except the guy who headed them appeared in my office looking for deals."

"Really," I asked intrigued, "what sort of deals?"

"Property finance ... big ... anything that we couldn't fund, or find a home for, he was interested in. Anyhow, we did a quick background check and found they were registered in the Caymans—with an unknown lawyer at the helm. That was Perez. We decided not to pursue a relationship. Then we heard they had gone international and were also funding some major property plays in New York City—a couple of billion worth."

"Then what?" I asked. "I've a feeling this story hasn't quite finished."

"They appointed a new man—very pushy. Perez remained in charge in the background, but the new guy took over up front. He was constantly ringing, calling in for a chat ...

annoying bastard, but I guess he had to get them in the game somehow. They apparently had billions to lend, according to him, but nobody could get a handle on the operation. He tried to get into some banks on Wall Street—I guess much the same as he did with me—but they got wise and blacklisted him and the company. Calima was around for maybe twelve months total, then they just shut down—supposed billions of dollars of deals one day, gone the next."

"Fascinating," I said, "David Perez and the vanishing billions. Well, I know where he is now, and there are apparently not too many billions within his current grasp. But if Alvarez was behind Calima, and maybe still is, that would explain their original money supply."

"Exactly," shot Tommy wheezing excitedly, "that's the connection between Perez and Alvarez."

"But tell me," I asked looking back to Dom, "who was the pushy bloke—the new one who was blacklisted?"

"Oh, him," said Dom looking to the ceiling as if trying to recall, "that's right, an Englishman who worked over here—*a guy called Paul Connolly*."

CHAPTER FORTY

I sat in my hotel room looking out at the Manhattan skyline. A million buildings of every size and shape. Just like the thoughts running through my head.

I now understood the relationship between Perez and Alvarez from the past. It was also pretty clear someone was trying to warn me off, and I had to assume it was Alvarez, as Tommy suggested. Well he, Alvarez, could get stuffed. I also had to assume that Perez was still under his control to some degree. Maybe total control!

But Connolly—he and Perez were still somehow tied together. Sure Connolly lived in a house controlled by Perez, but did the arrangement run deeper? And did he have a link directly to Alvarez? If he did, that would open a whole new range of possibilities, but Connolly would not admit to anything, particularly if a thug like Alvarez was controlling him.

My mind wandered back over the meetings, or more accurately encounters, I'd had with Connolly and Perez. The thing that struck me most was how nervous they were ... especially when I mentioned the names of others they may have been involved with. Okay, I'd concede my size could be intimidating, but neither was under direct physical threat from me at the time.

No, it was only at the mention of our three victims in Connolly's case, and the Alvarez name to Perez, that had both men visibly shaken. Neither would volunteer information on anybody else. Hell, they did their best to deny knowledge of anyone or anything associated with the others. My guess was that you could physically threaten them, and they still would reveal little, although everyone has a breaking point. Therefore, I concluded, the fear factor in their minds is real; particularly so if someone starts connecting the dots between them.

There had to be a more subtle approach, something that might convince them individually to open up a little. Each man had his weak points, his vulnerabilities, and I now had a couple on Perez. The time had come for a return visit to the Caymans, and a chance to explore the fine fractures in the Perez façade.

I called the airline and booked a flight to George Town for the following morning, then the Ritz Carlton for a room. It was getting late, but I wanted to thank Franch again ... I rang and offered him dinner. "Thanks buddy," he said, "I appreciate it, but I've made other plans. Let me know how you go, eh?"

One final thing to do ... at our last meeting in Union City, Manny had commented on the fondness of the drug lords for a retail presence; shopfronts that looked legit, but were just a cover. Franch had mentioned it too. It was a practice as old as Adam, but it occurred to me *that* might be a useful avenue for McClure to pursue, if he hadn't done so already. I knew there would be nobody at The Yard at that hour, so I left a message on Cindy's phone to have McClure call me in George Town the next day.

Now Mr Perez ... I smiled to myself at the thought of the next couple of days ... *let's see if we can improve your memory*.

CHAPTER
FORTY-ONE

I arrived in George Town around noon, and took a cab straight to the hotel. I noticed I had a missed call from Cindy . . . no doubt that was McClure getting back. I got to my room and dialled.

Cindy answered in her usual purring manner. God she sounded hot, and I so wanted to be with her. But there was work to do. "I'm back in the Caymans, to talk to this Perez goose again. Is McClure in?"

Apparently not—he always seemed to be out when I rang lately—so I got her to make sure he called me as soon as he returned. I then phoned Inspector Roberts and Marlene Rix to let them know I was back in the country. They were both, as usual, very courteous and offered their help any time.

I ordered lunch from room service, then set about to plan my next move with Perez. Do I just turn up unannounced at his office—the old surprise visit? No, he might not be there, so that would be wasted, and I might be seen anyway. Goodbye surprise! No, play it by the book—after all he is a goddamned lawyer— ring and make an appointment.

My phone rang. It was McClure. I chided him for being so hard to find, then quickly got him up to date with my New York and New Jersey activities. "So you see Jim, I'm hoping this might crack Perez... just a ray of light into his dealings will be a start."

"I agree Ash—probably the best move. But take care, won't you?"

I promised I would. "Oh, and one more thing—one of my contacts in the US suggested these Colombians love their retail front operations. You know, as a cover for their dope dealing or whatever. Don't know if your men have been looking, but I thought they should try and track down anything similar around where Sanchez was found. We might get lucky."

McClure agreed, although he believed that had been explored. Still, he promised to have his men look into it again. I then phoned the office of David Perez.

"Perez and Associates, David Perez speaking," answered the high-pitched male voice. It had a slightly prissy quality which I hadn't noticed before—maybe the mood at our earlier meeting was not so relaxed—anyway, this was unmistakably him.

"Todd, Australian Federal Police here," I announced as formally as possible. "I hope you've been keeping well since my last visit."

"F–fine thank you, what can I do for you?"

"I'd like to come and meet with you again tomorrow morning. I have some information that I think you might find interesting."

"R–really, what sort of i–information?"

"Far too delicate for me to discuss on the phone. Much better that we meet face-to-face. Shall we say ten o'clock ?"

"I think so—let me check my schedule," said Perez as he covered the mouthpiece of his phone. I could hear a muffled conversation, but couldn't make anything of it. Sounded like he had male company. Probably spot on, I smiled to myself.

"Yes," he drawled, as if thumbing slowly through the pages of a diary, "I think I could fit you in at about that time. I can see you at ten."

What crap, I thought—*could fit me in*—but I kept my calm . . . just play the game.

"Thank you, see you then," I said about to hang up, "oh, and by the way, that goon of yours, Jonas Toms, or any of his buddies—leave them at home, if you don't mind."

I then slowly closed off the call, but I knew he was still listening. *I could hear his quiet breathing.*

CHAPTER
FORTY-TWO

I don't know why but I felt a kind of peace descend on me after making the call to Perez. Maybe it's just the fear of the unknown in the call that causes a kind of nervousness, and once that's gone, the unknown that is, a sense of relief takes over. Whatever it was, that was how I felt as I sat on my room balcony, watching a couple of small catamarans dart back and forth across the blue-green ocean. Peaceful.

I had plenty of time to decide how to approach Perez, what to reveal and what to ask. Still, I found myself going over and over likely scenarios in my mind; what his reaction would be and how far I would really get with him. One thing was certain—I needed him to talk. Without that, there was no way I could make meaningful progress in this case.

My phone sprang to life which surprised me a bit—my new-found peace and a lazy Caribbean afternoon had lulled me into a trance-like state. I glanced at the screen and recognized a London prefix. "Todd," I answered adopting my formal tone again.

"Commander Todd, this is Jane Lau, you remember I am Andrew Lau's wife, from Hong Kong."

"Of course I do Mrs Lau, how are you keeping?"

"I'm okay, it's a bit lonely, but then Andrew was away so much I am fairly used to it, and two of my children are here, so we are coping."

"Yes, I understand. So—what can I do for you?"

"I am back in London now and have col-lected some of Andrew's belongings which the police were holding. I guess they were testing them, or whatever."

"Quite likely," I said, "what sort of belongings?"

"Just personal items—his wallet with credit cards and some cash, his watch and pen, and his mobile phone."

"So, was there a problem with them—something missing?"

"No, but I was pleased to have his phone. We have had to take over running the business, and I had no idea who he was talking to prior to his death. With the phone I can go back through the numbers and his contact list, and try to pick up where he was up to. Anyway, I found some numbers which did not match any of his contacts, so I thought I would call you."

"Yes," I said slowly, intrigued, "why would these numbers have any interest for me?"

"Would you like me to give them to you—can you take them down?"

I grabbed a pen and notepad. "Okay—what are they?"

Mrs Lau proceeded to read three numbers, carefully going over each three times to make sure I had them down correctly. The first two appeared to be London city numbers, and the third I wasn't sure. "So these are not regular clients of your husband?" I asked.

"Not at all. The first number he called the day before he died. The next two he called just a couple of hours before. They were not in the contacts list, so I was a bit curious. I dialled the one beginning with 33—that is a French number I believe—and an Englishman answered."

"Really, did he give a name?"

"No, and when I told him who I was, he hung up. But my guess is it was that Mr Connolly. You remember I told you they had spoken a few times before?"

"Yes, that would fit—Connolly does live in France. But what about the other two numbers—did you try them?"

"Not the one from the day before," continued Mrs Lau. "I really wanted to know who he had spoken to before he died, so I tried that one first. Then I definitely did not try after that one. I was too confused Commander, and that is why I thought I should call you."

"Go on," I said, now totally engrossed and probably more confused than Mrs Lau, "what about the last one?"

"That's what I found really strange, and I hope you can find something out. Just an hour or so before Andrew was shot he called that number—*it was to Scotland Yard.*"

CHAPTER
FORTY-THREE

W hy on earth would Andrew Lau be calling Scotland Yard... unless he had an imminent problem of course? But no evidence had come to light that he had *any* sort of problem. The doormen at The Landmark, where he and Walker were murdered, reported that he appeared in high spirits as he entered the hotel.

His lifestyle was one of considerable wealth; a man who had established and run a very successful import and export business for more than thirty years. Fashion items mostly—handbags and the like. An operation which spanned Asia, Australia, and Europe, with offices in Hong Kong, Sydney, and

London, and substantial homes in each of those cities.

His wife, Jane, was a few years his junior and had spent her early life in Singapore. She completed her education there, which gave her a solid grounding of English customs, and moved to Hong Kong at twenty-one when she and Andrew married. He was rising quickly in finance with Standard Chartered Bank, having completed his degree at the London School of Economics.

Their future looked bright; they had three children and Andrew rose quickly through the bank, but his spirit was entrepreneurial. Banking was too restrictive for him, and in his late-twenties an opportunity came to buy into the business of one of his clients—a small Hong Kong exporter. He grabbed it with both hands, and within five years he owned the whole show.

Jane was his rock behind-the-scenes. Like many Asian women, she was happy to look after the home and raise the children, but he always sought her view on important business decisions. No venture was undertaken, no new product line introduced, no borrowing agreed to, without it being discussed with Jane.

And that's why I found it strange that, according to his wife, Andrew Lau was potentially hooking up in a business deal with Ernesto Alvarez. "Partners," she had said. Particularly as she apparently had no idea what the deal was—or if she did, she wasn't letting on. This needed some attention.

Jane Lau had said she would be in London for the next week or so, attending to her late husband's business. I arranged to meet with her once I returned. But first things first—tomorrow morning, *David Perez was expecting me.*

CHAPTER FORTY-FOUR

I bounded up the stairs to the Perez office smack on the dot of ten o'clock. No point keeping him waiting, and I *just knew* he was bursting to see me. Not!

Two quick raps on the door, and I flung it open without waiting for a reply. David Perez was looking at me intently, but he remained seated, firmly ensconced behind his desk. I guessed he viewed it as some form of protection, some barrier no matter how small. I glanced around the room, but there was no one else present. At least he appeared to have kept that part of the bargain.

"Have a seat," he said unsmilingly, indicating a brown vinyl armchair opposite his desk.

"Thank you, but I'll stand," I replied. I always felt it gave me a more commanding presence if I stood—particularly when the other person chose to remain seated. Mind games maybe, but they had a long way to go to get up to my level. Physically speaking, that is.

"What do you want this time?" asked Perez somewhat sternly, and glaring at me.

"I want to know who killed Andrew Lau and Terry Walker. Do you know?" I asked equally briskly, and stared hard back at him. If Perez was going to be abrupt with me, then I would return the favour.

"N–no I don't," he replied looking down at his lap, the nervousness returning. That didn't take long. The façade was slipping already.

"Then let's try this for size," I continued, "I know you ran Calima Ministries in New York for Ernesto Alvarez." I turned my back on him and, hands in pockets, deliberately strolled to the end of his office, then turned and faced him again.

"I know the operation had nothing to do with religion, that you were offering interna-tional finance deals." Hands still in pockets, I strolled back towards him. Perez couldn't direct his gaze away from me far enough, but he had little option. He still said nothing.

I pushed a bit further. "I know Paul Connolly worked for you at Calima—he was your front man for the money. So don't get cute with me about whether you may, or may not, have ever met him. I also know you didn't settle any of your deals. You, Calima and Connolly disappeared—pulled the plug. Why was that Mr Perez?"

"I–I am not really sure . . ." he stammered.

By now I was standing at his desk, towering over him. "Bullshit!" I thundered, and slammed both fists down hard. Perez jumped in his chair and looked plainly terrified, as a bundle of folders and pens hit the floor. I turned away again, and stood with my back to him in silence.

"Th–the money supply was pulled," said Perez slowly, turning in his chair to look out the window. "I swear I don't know who p–pulled it—who made the decision—I was just told one day that all deals were off. We had so many deals written, and so many big clients waiting, and we had to walk away from all of them."

"Right," I said jumping in, "so you *now* admit that you know Connolly, that he was part of it?"

"Yes, I know him," he sighed, as though a great weight had been released.

"So, why do you have him lodging in a property you control?"

"I don't really have any say in that—it's not up to me, I just manage it."

"Manage it for *who*?"

Perez was starting to look terrified again. "For some people—I am not able to say, it's not worthwhile..." and his voice trailed off. For Christ sake, I thought, this bloke takes weak-kneed and lily-livered to a whole new level. Time to push harder.

"Mr Perez, let me be perfectly clear about what else I know. I am aware of your relation-ship with the past Chief Justice, and of the nature of your sexual liaisons here. I know that you remain in the Cayman Islands only on the say so of the Governor and that if this were to become public knowledge, your ten-ure here would be over."

Perez was *stunned.* His face reddened and he started to tremble, then put his head in his hands and his whole body shook. "H–how did you find . . .?"

"Not important," I said, "it's my job to discover these things. Now perhaps in order to maintain your current standing in the community, you might like to reveal what you know about the murders of Lau and Walker."

"N–nothing; nothing at all. They were clients of Calima, that's all. Until you came, I swear I didn't know they were dead. B–but you could try Connolly—he is always still trying to do money deals. He might know something, might have been in touch with them."

"He's not very talkative, but if you give me a bit more on him I'll give him another try. So, what's the deal with Connolly?"

Perez hesitated slightly. "He took the fall for us. When we bailed out of the deals, people were very unhappy and came gunning for us. Those at the top organised Connolly to take the rap. He did five years, and now has the lifestyle you've seen . . . his compensation. As I said before, I have nothing else to do with it— just manage it."

"I assume by *those at the top* you mean Alvarez?"

Perez turned to look out the window again. He sat in silence for a moment, then shook his head. "I can't say any more."

"As you wish, just remember what I know about you. I *will* get to the bottom of these murders, and if you become collateral damage, so be it."

I turned to leave and dropped my card on his desk. At least I now knew the deal with Connolly, direct from the person who oversees his surprisingly comfortable lifestyle, and that he may still be dealing with his old money clients. I opened the door and turned back to face Perez. He looked shattered, defeated.

"By the way," I said, almost as an afterthought, "you remember there was a third person murdered at about the same time . . . she was tied up with Walker. I don't suppose you know her—name was Juanita Sanchez?"

Perez started trembling again, buried his head in his hands and began to cry uncontrollably.

"Oh, my God, no, no, no," he sobbed, "they didn't tell me, no, no, it cannot be . . . *she is my sister.*"

CHAPTER
FORTY-FIVE

F rankly I was glad to be out of the Perez office, and not just because of the depressing décor. His life was unravelling before his eyes, partly because of me, but then mostly it had to do with Perez himself or those in his circle. I was just the bearer of bad news—not the cause. Still, delivering the message his sister had been terminated was unpleasant... if accidental. I guessed, from his reaction, we could eliminate him as a suspect in that one... but I didn't want to be there watching him disintegrate. Hell, I might even begin to feel sorry for him.

At least I hadn't come away empty-handed. I now had the confirmation I needed that Alvarez controlled all the entities managed by Perez, including Connolly. Sure Perez stopped short of actually telling me that Alvarez was behind everything; the fear was just too great, but it wasn't hard to read between the lines. Sometimes, I guess, what is unsaid is stronger than the spoken word.

But if Connolly was living the high life courtesy of Alvarez, albeit quietly, then I was willing to bet that involved some form of IOU in the opposite direction. Okay, Connolly had taken the fall for the team, and five years inside was a solid price to pay. The flipside is that he now lived the life of a multi-multi. My gut said Alvarez would still require *something* from him for the privilege. Proving it might take a little more work.

I headed back to my hotel to arrange flights as soon as I could—back to London as a first stop. Depending on how McClure's team had fared, I might have some more delving to do there. And I needed to meet up with Jane Lau. Then there was Connolly—he would probably require a follow-up visit as well. I couldn't imagine he would respond to a phone call. And Cindy—*I could taste her already.*

CHAPTER
FORTY-SIX

E rnesto Alvarez was livid. He rarely expressed his anger openly, finding it much more effective to maintain an external aura of calm, whilst coldly-calculating each move. That included revenge or even death, if need be. He paced the vast marble-floored living room of his penthouse, phone pressed firmly to his ear.

"That is absolutely fucking unbelievable. I can't imagine it. David, you leave it to me—we'll get to the bottom of *this*," he bellowed down the line.

His life was one of control. Control of product supply lines into the United Kingdom, control of those who distributed for him, control of various individuals in positions of influence who helped ensure that his distribution continued, unhindered, and control of anybody who got in his way.

To a large degree he even controlled the supply source. It used to be Rodriguez, but he was now dead courtesy of the Colombian police and a rival outfit. Now the Rodriguez family, or more specifically his two sons, had control of the empire, and Alvarez with forty years of cunning behind him, could usually manage to get whatever he wanted from them.

This time, however, control seemed to be slipping away. This damn copper, Todd, couldn't be nailed down. First he's roughed up Connolly, who's a nervous bastard at the best of times. By all reports this commander was a huge man, fit and strong, and he was lucky Connolly held himself together long enough to get away from him, without spilling too much.

Then the clowns in New Jersey screwed up big time. *Amateurs!* The instructions were to extract information from Todd, at least enough so Alvarez could anticipate his next move . . . his likely line of attack. Maybe even frighten him off.

Failing that, Todd was to be left with sufficient pain and suffering... a few broken
bones, some bruising... enough to slow him
down a touch. *Kill the incentive*. Instead, the
copper had delivered back to Alvarez *no*
information, and two men with smashed-up
heads who were now useless to the operation.
And *they* now knew too much, so they would
have to be dealt with *differently*.

This commander had some good help.
Alvarez didn't know who these people were,
those who'd rescued him, but the three of
them together, out back of that liquor shop in
Union City, were more than a match for anybody he had on that side of the Atlantic. Short
of using a gun, of course.

On top of that, they had sent him a message from Tommy. A *"fuck you"* message.

That damn Tommy Garcia would be the
only person in Union City who would have the
balls to do that. God only knew how Todd
originally got to Garcia, but it meant his
informants were good.

Worse, Todd had paid a return visit to
Perez. Perez was now on the phone in a hell of
a state, stuttering and crying that Todd
nailed him and his past problems in the

Caymans. If Todd went public with the information, Perez was gone. He would be forced to leave immediately and had nowhere else to go.

On top of all this, Perez now knew his older sister had been killed, and nobody had bothered to tell him. He was distraught; wanted to know what Alvarez knew about it. Who had killed her? Why was she killed? The questions came like a Gatling gun.

Alvarez intensely disliked being questioned in this manner. Naturally, he denied any knowledge. How could he admit to his long-term employee that he had ordered the hit on his sister? Why *would* he admit it? Not his style.

No, Alvarez did not like receiving these calls. This was not how he did business. Everyone in his food chain was vulnerable. They all carried baggage, Alvarez included, and Todd was beginning to exploit it.

There was no doubt—Ernesto Alvarez felt he was losing control—*and it was making him as mad as hell.*

CHAPTER
FORTY-SEVEN

My flight from JFK to Heathrow landed at about seven a.m. As usual the customs and baggage collection was quick, proving yet again, the advantages of being a federal law enforcer. It didn't stop the way I felt however; thirty-six hours of travelling from my departure in George Town had left me feeling unwashed and washed out.

I took a taxi to my hotel, showered and dressed, and got ready for some more detective legwork. This time, however, I'd booked my own hotel. It's funny how little things stick in your mind, and something Lanfranchi had said kept gnawing at me—the fact that others often seem to know your movements, and you can never really pinpoint how they know. Or words to that effect.

The incident at the Alvarez-controlled liquor shop in Union City drove the point home. Much better if I remained independent, and told nobody... as far as possible... where I was staying. On that basis, I was now comfortably settled into The Landmark. What better place, *than the scene of the crime?*

I put in a couple of calls—firstly to McClure's office to let him know of my return. As usual, Cindy took the call. It was so good to hear her voice and be back in the same town. I arranged a time to meet with McClure the following morning. I also arranged dinner with her for that evening.

"At your hotel," she asked, "where are you staying?"

"With friends," I lied, thinking quickly and remembering she had told me she lived near Covent Garden, "some old friends in Soho suggested I stay with them, so I took them up on the offer. Maybe there is an okay restaurant somewhere nearby?"

"Well I live only a few minutes from there, so why don't you come here and I'll cook for you?"

It was an offer too good to refuse—she gave me her address and we set a date for seven.

My second call was to Jane Lau at the company office, as we had agreed on her call to me in George Town. We arranged a meeting for two o' clock that afternoon.

Now, I thought, let's see if dead men really do tell tales.

CHAPTER
FORTY-EIGHT

The Lau empire—or more correctly the Wujing Trading Company—operated from a pair of industrial units in the suburb of Hounslow, close to Heathrow airport. The sort of bland but functional buildings ... warehouse at ground level and offices above ... which were now standard fare in every light industrial business park. Pity I didn't know the Lau office was here earlier. It would have saved me the return trip from the city.

I climbed the flight of stairs to the office level and was greeted by a young Asian receptionist. Chinese I assumed, but from her accent I would guess she had lived her entire life in London. She very politely offered me tea and ushered me into a side office deco-rated in pale blue, and complete with marble-top boardroom table surrounded by about a dozen leather armchairs.

Jane Lau appeared a few minutes later, we shook hands and I offered her my condolences again. A pretty, immaculately groomed woman, she looked younger than her sixty years—maybe ten years younger. Despite her loss, she was remarkably composed and to the point.

"Thank you for coming Commander. I hope I don't disappoint you if I do not appear emotional and distraught, but our culture does not encourage it in public. Truth is, Andrew and I had a very good marriage, but as I mentioned before we spent much of our recent past in different cities. I had become used to not having him around, but I was still very much involved with the business behind the scenes. Except obviously for these new people we have discussed—I've had no knowledge or dealing with them at all."

We drank our tea and I asked her various questions about the business, the products they traded, its profitability and so on. Her answers were forthright, and there appeared nothing unremarkable, except that the business was obviously very lucrative and had been so for a long time.

"A little over ten years ago your husband sought a loan from Paul Connolly, which we have discussed, but do you know what it was for?" I asked.

"That was for a property development deal, which was outside normal business, but Andrew thought it was so good he wanted to take it on. And he kept saying the money on offer was such a good deal too."

"You said he has been in touch again with Connolly, and the phone records support that. You also said he mentioned 'being in business' with Alvarez. Was he pursuing any property this time?"

"Not that I know of—he wouldn't necessarily tell me if he was considering something, but I'm sure he would if he had decided to buy it. I can't imagine what this business with Alvarez, whoever he is, could be."

"The less you know about him, the better," I replied, "but I can assure you, business with Alvarez would be less than savoury. It may appear okay at the outset, but it would end badly. Actually, it already has."

There was a knock at the door and a Chinese man entered the room. I guessed he was about thirty, dressed in denim jeans and open neck shirt and carrying a blue folder. He looked quite fidgety.

"Commander," said Mrs Lau, "meet my son Thomas."

I stood and we shook hands, but Thomas was distracted, as though he urgently wanted to tell his mother something and my presence was interfering. She sensed his anxiety.

"Thomas is our marketing manager here—he knows all about handbags, belts and shoes—but now he has to learn about finance. It's okay Thomas, the commander is here to help us so you can tell me what is worrying you."

Thomas looked at me briefly, then back at his mother. He slowly drew a sheet of paper and some bank statements from his folder, and placed them on the table.

"I have been going through our financial records covering the past three or four months, trying to get a handle on our cash flow. It's a bit of a paper war Commander. My father didn't like electronic records, so we wait until the end of each month for these physical bank statements to arrive. Anyway it all looked quite normal—regular purchases and regular sales—that is until about three weeks ago."

This piqued my interest. Abnormalities and murders often go hand in hand.

"What do you call 'normal'?" I asked.

Thomas again looked at his mother, and she smiled and nodded for him to continue.

"We make purchases of about £5 million a month."

"That's substantial," I said, "good for a private company. What about sales?"

Thomas looked a bit embarrassed. "About £7 million a month."

I let out a low whistle. "That is impressive—40% margin and £2 million a month profit. So what changed three weeks ago?"

"Well," continued Thomas, "it appears my father opened another bank account, our fifth, and under a new company name, but it is still part of the Wujing group. Three weeks ago the new company made a purchase of £7 million in its own right. Much bigger than normal."

"You know what the money was for—what was purchased?" I asked.

"No idea, but the sales proceeds came in within two days of the purchase. For £8.5 million."

"Pretty impressive turnaround, that sort of profit in a couple of days. I assume that's not standard performance in the accessory industry?"

Both mother and son shook their heads. Jane Lau looked decidedly startled.

"Out of left field," I asked, "you don't know who the payments went to, and came from, by any chance?"

"I do," continued Thomas, "I had the bank look into it as it was so strange. The payments went through the same bank in the Cayman Islands. As far as I know we have never done business there before. In the Caymans, that is. The payment we made was to a company called Turbo Investments, and the one we received was *from a Soacha Capital.*"

CHAPTER
FORTY-NINE

The return trip to the city was certainly thought-provoking after my meeting at Wujing Trading. This time I took a local Hounslow taxi, on the advice of Jane Lau. Half the cost of a black cab.

What to make of this connection between Andrew Lau and Alvarez? What did Andrew Lau mean when he told his wife he was 'in business' with Alvarez? Partners? Surely he hadn't moved into drug trafficking! He had a substantial business; no, he had a bloody fabulous business. He made more in a year than most people would make in several lifetimes. Why risk it fooling around with drugs?

If he was in business with Alvarez, then why was he killed? Even if Lau had entered the narcotics world, he was hardly some seedy street dealer. He might not have the experience of it that Alvarez possessed, but my guess is that he would only go into something on an equal footing. So why would Alvarez kill him, or have him killed? That is, assuming Alvarez *was* responsible.

True, Alvarez was a murdering bastard. But he didn't murder people just for the hell of it. As powerful as he was, he didn't need unwanted attention. Part of his control was that business was to be conducted quietly and efficiently, with all parties paid as agreed. Retribution, when it was needed, was always quick, decisive, and as private as possible. What was the saying? *Blood on the streets is bad for business*. He didn't go round shooting people for practice. No, if Alvarez had ordered the hit on Lau, there had to be a strong underlying reason. Whatever their *business* was, some falling out had occurred.

I got back to The Landmark and phoned Sally back in Sydney. It had been days since I had tried to ring her, and I felt as though I had been halfway round the world in that time. So much had happened. She seemed pleased to hear from me, which was a nice change, but as usual my call coincided with her leaving for work, and she *had to go*. I always felt empty after these calls—we never seemed to actually discuss anything—and there were *other distractions* on my doorstep. No wonder long-distance affairs were so damn hard.

Well, I thought, make the best of what you've got now, and deal with the rest later. So I showered and changed; best denims, splashed on a little cologne, double-pocket shirt with my initials embroidered on the left, and best boots ... and readied myself for dinner with the delectable Cindy.

CHAPTER FIFTY

I took a taxi from the front of the hotel and we set off along Marylebone Road for Covent Garden. Charles, the duty manager, had given me directions for the address, but I didn't want to pull up outside her apartment block in the cab—after all I was supposedly staying less than a ten-minute walk away. So I had the driver drop me outside the Covent Garden Tube, and set off on foot for the remaining two or three blocks.

I found her building—an old three or four storey converted warehouse—and located the unit number on the security intercom. I was just about to buzz it when my phone rang. Cindy was calling.

"Ash, honey," she purred, "are you on your way yet?"

"I am—in fact I'm right outside your front door."

"Ohhh, I'm so sorry. I have to go back to work and I've only just found out. There's no way I'll be done here for hours yet. I feel dreadful doing this to you, but I don't know what else to do. Can we reschedule? I hope you'll forgive me."

I must admit it was a bit of a letdown. I'd been mentally preparing for this moment, to hold and touch her, for days on end, but what could I do? And she genuinely sounded sorry.

"Of course babe, don't worry about it. Of all people I understand the industry, so I can imagine the position you're in. I'm enjoying the sights, so I'll just continue my journey. We've got a meeting scheduled for the morning... I'll see you then."

"Thank you for being so understanding," she said. "I can't wait to see you tomorrow."

Well, that had flattened out the evening. What to do now? I glanced up and down the street which was busy, vibrant. Maybe a bit touristy, but what a great place to land in. Full of life. Hell, *I* was a tourist. Across the street, maybe forty or fifty yards away, the corner pub was buzzing; people standing outside on the footpath, drinking in the warm evening air. I hadn't noticed it as I concentrated on finding Cindy's place. The Crown and Anchor it said—that sounded like me—I made a bee-line for it.

I settled at a table in an upstairs bar overlooking the street, ordered a pint of ale—Harvey's Best—and sausages and mash. English pub food, that's what I needed. Reminded me of home! I sat and listened, and watched the world swirl around me.

I was enjoying the evening's viewing when my phone trilled again. It was Lanfranchi calling from New York. "Hey Franch, what's up? Everything OK? "

"Ash, all's good, hope you're looking after yourself. You in London?"

"Uh-huh, got in this morning."

"I'll be quick—Tommy called me with something he thought might be useful for you . . . to do with Alvarez. He said he's found a connection that you should follow—a company called Providencia Investment. Hope it helps. Anyway, gotta go. Let me know how you get on."

"Thanks Franch, I'll get on it. Oh, hey . . . thank Tommy for me will you?" And he was gone.

CHAPTER
FIFTY-ONE

Well, it had been a long road without much of a turn. Maybe this would give us a break, but I'd have to get someone in The Yard to check it up for me. That would have to wait until morning. Time to leave; I decided to walk back to the hotel. I guessed it would take maybe thirty minutes, the evening was pleasant ... cooling down a little ... and I would get to see more of London.

I set off checking out the shops, the bars, the nightlife, and heading in what I hoped was the right direction. I crossed over Charing Cross Road and figured if I took the back streets, I could short cut my way to Oxford Street. It was then a simple matter of following along to Marble Arch, turn right and presto, straight through to The Landmark.

I travelled about half a dozen blocks and crossed to a narrow street which was a mixture of old terraces and some commercial buildings. I was aware of a car coming down the street behind me, but took little notice. As I reached the footpath, the car suddenly accelerated hard, tyres screeching. I glanced back and realised it was coming *at me*. In a split second I jumped away from it and smashed heavily into a brick wall. The force of the impact stunned me for a moment, and I slumped to hands and knees on the pavement.

The car stopped about fifty yards along the street, then reversed hard, tyres screaming again, screeching to a stop beside me where I was still slumped on the ground. I could feel a warm trickle of blood running down the side of my face, and reached in under my jacket for my Glock. This had the potential to *get ugly*.

The driver's window slid down and someone . . . the driver maybe . . . produced a pistol which was pointed at the side of my head, about three inches away. Funny, in all the possible scenarios which had run through my mind in the course of this job, I had never thought of dying in a narrow street somewhere in Soho. I decided to leave my gun where it was.

The rear passenger window of the car lowered slowly, and a male voice spoke. "For your own safety, Commander Todd, finish your investigation *now*! *Leave the country*!"

I squinted up at the window, but I couldn't make out who was speaking. The car was dark with tinted windows. European looking, possibly a Beemer or Mercedes. Whatever—it was dark and the street was dark. There was only a faint glow from a nearby light on the opposite side of the street.

As the window was raised and the car moved off, this time quietly, I caught a glimpse of somebody in the passenger seat, on the far side. They were illuminated by the street light, and it made me gasp. Surely not—no, it couldn't be. Maybe it was the head knock and I wasn't seeing properly, but it gave me a start.

In that fleeting moment, the profile of the person in the passenger seat looked *just like Cindy*.

CHAPTER FIFTY-TWO

I slowly hauled myself to my feet brushing off the London street grit, and mopped the blood from my face with my handkerchief. There seemed to be plenty of it judging from the mess it made. I continued walking towards Oxford Street, trying to make some sense of what had just occurred.

The threat, from whoever it was, I could deal with. Two things were certain; I would *not* finish my investigation now, and I would *not leave the country*! It was the thought of Cindy being in the car that kept playing over and over in my mind. But was it *really* her? She was at work, *wasn't she*?

Once I reached Oxford Street I figured I might as well keep on walking. The area was packed with night-time revellers, and I was attracting plenty of attention, given my bloodied state. But I guessed no self-respecting cabbie would want to take me; I'd just look like too much trouble. So I strode on, or more accurately, staggered on.

The questions kept coming—if the car which just hit me belonged to Alvarez, how did they know where I was? And if it was Alvarez, or his henchmen, what was Cindy doing with *them*? If it *was Cindy*. Too many *ifs* for my aching head!

I finally reached The Landmark, and Charles the duty manager greeted me at the front desk. "Good evening Commander, are you all right? What has happened? Can I help?"

"Thanks Charles, just a slight accident but I'll be okay. You wouldn't have anything I can clean this up with, would you?"

"Yes, of course," said Charles, "I'll fetch something and bring it to your room in a few minutes."

True to his word Charles arrived about five minutes later, carrying copious quantities of bandages, cotton wool, antiseptic and a pair of scissors. "Let me fix it for you Commander, first aid is part of our training here," he said. Which he did, and a good job of it too. Much better than any patch up I might have attempted.

Charles finished applying the strip, and packed the remaining medical supplies. As he prepared to leave, he hesitated for just a second. "Commander, are you working or are you just on holiday?"

"I'm not at liberty to say, Charles, we don't comment on anything. Why do you ask?"

"Sorry . . . I didn't mean to be rude, but a few weeks ago there was a murder here in our hotel. In fact it was a double murder. I just thought, by coincidence, you might be looking at it. But if not . . ."

"No," I said cutting in, "I didn't think you were being rude. Why, do you know something about it?"

"N–no, not really, not about the actual murder. It's just . . ." and he hesitated again.

"Just?" I gave him a quizzical look, one eyebrow raised.

He let out a big sigh. "Just that a strange thing happened recently. Well, today really."

"Yes?" This was like pulling teeth.

"Well, I was on duty the evening after the murder, and we had a video in the safe taken by our closed-circuit cameras. I haven't seen the footage, but the duty manager before me told me that it covered the foyer, the lifts and the corridor to the room where it happened."

"Interesting, is it still there now? Could I have a look at it?"

"That's the strange thing," continued Charles, "the other duty manager told me the police who came to investigate, asked him to put it in there. It's been there all this time, until this evening. And now it's gone, *on my watch*!"

"So you have no idea who took it—you didn't see anyone go to the safe?"

"No. I'm sure it was there when I came on duty at about six. The only other person with access to the safe is the previous duty manager, and he left at about eight."

"Which way did he leave?" I asked.

"We all come and go via a rear entrance. The lobby is for guests; not staff."

"Do your cameras cover the safe and the corridors leading to the rear entrance?"

"Yes, I think so," said Charles, "and I believe they would also cover the rear street."

Bingo! "Charles, I'll let you in on a little secret, just between us—I *am* looking at this case—and it would be a great help if you could get me a camera footage of all those areas, say between six and nine tonight. And please don't give them to anyone else—only me. Great work—I could make a detective of you yet."

Charles beamed. "Absolutely sir—for your eyes only and I'll have them here as fast as I can."

He strode purposefully out of the room, and I was sure he saluted as he closed the door.

CHAPTER
FIFTY-THREE

The next morning was grey, overcast, and much colder. "Showers likely," said the weather presenter on the breakfast news. Funny how fast the weather changes here. Great one day, miserable the next ten.

True to his word, Charles had brought the videos to me. Well, copies anyway. He had to identify the footage I required, and had then made DVD's of each on his own computer. "Don't forget to erase it," I reminded him, "we don't have a court order for this, so we don't want someone discovering you have them on your system, do we? The less explaining we have to do, the better."

It had taken him some time and was after midnight when he delivered them. I spent the next three hours scanning disc after disc, so I was dog tired. Still I needed to be up and going—I had a meeting with McClure to attend. But boy, were those videos fruitful!

Naturally, they showed the various comings and goings of staff members. Nothing unusual in any of that. A couple of minutes after eight, as Charles had said, a staff member who I assumed must be the earlier duty manager, left the hotel via the rear entrance door.

On a separate video covering the street, a large, dark Mercedes was parked a few feet along from the door. I couldn't make out a numberplate, but the forensic people could fix that. The driver . . . solid and powerfully built, wearing a suit and gloves . . . left the car and started talking to the now, off-duty manager. He was obviously expecting them.

Both men then entered the hotel. The corridor video showed them walking towards the safe room. The third video, in the room which housed the safe, showed the duty manager open the safe and retrieve a small parcel, which he handed to the driver.

The pair then left by the rear door, the driver returning to the wheel and the manager turning in the opposite direction. The passenger window slid down, and the manager spoke briefly to whoever was inside. Too dark to tell from the footage. Could either man be Alvarez, I wondered? No, not the driver; he was too young, probably only about forty. If I could get a fix on the plate later, that might nail it down.

One thing was certain—I now had living proof that the security in the hotel had been compromised. A duty manager was caught, on-camera, interfering with police evidence. But why had the police left the evidence there for so long? A thought occurred to me— maybe they had no court order either! But why? Why not use official channels? I decided to take a leaf from their book, and hang on to my video evidence. No rush for them ... no rush for me.

The problem for the duty manager was that in time, he would be charged, unless he could supply a damn good reason for his action—like the *threat of death;* perhaps. A bigger problem for him though, if it *was* the

Alvarez camp he was dealing with, the threat was likely to be *real*.

CHAPTER
FIFTY-FOUR

I arrived at the Met office a few minutes before nine, and endured the usual grilling by ground floor security, before the smiles returned and I was ushered to the lift, and the fifth floor which housed McClure's office.

Cindy was waiting outside for me. She kept the moment formal by offering her hand, which I shook, making sure I held it with *both* hands. She glanced around quickly, then looked at me with those beautiful brown eyes and whispered, "what happened to you—your head? Sorry about dinner last night—I'll talk to you later. The DCI is ready."

I entered the office with Cindy following. His right hand man DI Carty was seated near the window and McClure stoically ensconced behind his giant desk. He rose and greeted me warmly.

"Great to see you Ash. It feels from here as though you've been around the world. How did you get on... and your head—what gives?"

"Interesting Jim... been to a few places I *never knew existed*, and learnt *new* things," I replied, feigning mock excitement.

Carty's demeanour made me slightly uneasy though. I couldn't put a finger on it—he didn't stand, or offer his hand, when I arrived—which I find downright rude. In fact, the two of them looked like they were estab-lished members of the '*old boys club*' and I was the outsider. So I covered, in general terms, where I'd been and what I found. For the moment I thought I'd keep my few, vital secrets, well... secret... tell them what they *needed* to know.

They all nodded wisely as I described my meetings with the NYPD, the Cayman police and David Perez. I even told them about Tommy Garcia and Jane Lau, but with no details.

"So I've got bugger all in the way of suspects. And this," I said pointing to my wound, "I don't know but somebody last night tried to run me over. At least that's how it appeared, and I hit my head getting out of the way. They warned me off—told me to get out of town. No idea *who* they were." I glanced across at Cindy, but she stared at her notepad ... not a flicker from her. The others just shook theirs in sympathy—but not too much I noticed. What I also noticed, was no offer came from either officer to help track down whoever attacked me.

We exchanged a few more pleasantries, including a quick discussion on the merits of the English and Australian cricket teams, but the meeting was running out of ideas. Obviously, The Yard had nothing further to add—whether they knew anything or not, they weren't telling—and I was actively *withholding information.* "I'll get going Jim, there are a couple of minor items I'll chase up, see if they take us anywhere. But if not, I'm running out of leads ... just like the original investigation, dying on the vine."

"Well Ash, you've done a great job to date, and if this is where it ends, then so be it. I can keep the team following it from here. Let me know how you get on with these other leads, then we'll review the whole enquiry."

That *stunned* me! In a little over a fortnight I had been feted as a saviour for The Yard in taking on this case at short notice, been belted, tortured, all but run down—twice, and now it was all "lovely to see you and thanks for coming."

Well, if that was the official line, they could go to hell—I'd make my own arrangements. I didn't know about the others, but I felt Jane Lau deserved better than this. As a matter of fact, *so did I.*

I rose to leave and reached over and shook the hand of DI Carty, who remained seated. I gripped it *hard*, and he winced, apparently in some pain. "Sorry," I said, smiling apologetically. But it felt *good*.

I opened the door and turned back to face the two men. "By the way Jim, you remember I asked if your team could check any Colombian businesses around where the Sanchez woman was found? Any luck?"

McClure looked vague, and seemed to avoid my gaze. "No, nothing further at all on that front."

I nodded my understanding, and left the meeting. All pretty unsatisfactory really ... this shrug of the shoulders, going nowhere approach. At that moment I began to wonder if Scotland Yard *really was* interested in solving this case. Or were they just *running dead*?

CHAPTER
FIFTY-FIVE

I walked between the rows of desks, and on the far side of the vast floor I noticed Sergeant Shepherd at his desk. I had a sudden urge to talk to him... a gut feeling that he was one person I could trust. *An honest, old-fashioned copper.*

We exchanged greetings. "Sergeant, have you been working on these murders since I left?"

"No, not really. No new information so there hasn't been much to follow-up, only paperwork and more bloody paperwork," he replied dourly.

"Well, three things—first, there was a credit card used by our suspects, at the hotel.

It seems to have been forgotten. Any news on it?"

"Yes sir, there was. Held in the name of Raelene Kater, like the licence. Bank approved the charge, and then it seems the customer disputed it. Now the subject of a bank and hotel work-out. Not that we think she actually exists, mind ... just another dodgy job, looks like."

"That figures. Okay, second—this number," I said, producing a slip of paper from my pocket, "belongs to here. Lau called it shortly before he was killed ... do you recognise it?"

"General line sir—into this unit though, I think."

"So it's not direct?"

"No," said the sergeant, looking over the number again, "anyone here could have picked up the call. We could trace it—might take some time."

"Don't worry ... third, would you be able check something for me—and tell *nobody*, including *anyone* here?"

"Of course—half the time I tell them things and I don't think they take any notice anyhow ... like the credit card ... so it won't be much different, will it?"

"Excellent. Could you get onto the companies register here ... not sure what they call it."

"Companies House it's called," he cut in.

"Yes, could you get onto Companies House and check out a firm called Providencia Investment? Find out everything you can ... directors, names and addresses, major shareholders, anything. But particularly, a list of assets—what they own—that's what I really want to know."

"No problem Commander, happy to oblige. Will give me something different to think about," replied the sergeant.

I handed him my card, thanked him and made for the lifts. As I turned the corner, there was Cindy. "This is becoming our usual meeting place—pity we couldn't find somewhere with a little more atmosphere," I said, smiling.

"Why don't we fix that tonight," she said, "let's try again, my place, same time?"

"Done," I said, and stepped into the lift.

CHAPTER
FIFTY-SIX

I retreated to the comparative safety of my room at The Landmark. I wanted to go over the footage Charles had given me again, to make absolutely sure I hadn't missed anything, and see once and for all if I could identify anyone else in them. It had been a very bleary and tired viewing session in the early hours of this morning, and I could use some more sleep!

As I passed through the lobby I noticed the manager on duty—it had to be the same young man as in my discs. Same fair curly hair, late-twenties maybe. The one, it seemed, Alvarez now had his hooks into. My natural reaction was to warn him of the danger he was in. But I couldn't—that would risk a tip-off to Alvarez—so I kept right on walking. It still didn't sit well though.

I turned on the television, popped the DVD in the player, pressed the button and settled back to watch the action. Definitely the same young duty manager I had just seen downstairs. The images were slightly grainy, and the movement of staff a little jerky, a bit like an old computer game, but I determined to watch it all again.

My phone sprang to life. Strange, I had just been watching two female staff members walking towards the rear door, and now the driver from the dark Mercedes was coming through with the duty manager. What was going on? Then I noticed the time—two hours had elapsed. I must have fallen asleep.

"Yes?" I answered cautiously.

"Shepherd here sir," said the voice on the other end, "with the results of your enquiry."

"Oh … thanks Sergeant, what did you find?"

"Well sir, a number of things. First, there was only one director, Juanita Sanchez, and the registered office is a law firm in the city. That's our victim I believe sir, the one we're investigating."

"Very interesting, so their only director is dead. No replacement yet! What else?"

"Major shareholders appear to be companies—I haven't done any follow up on them—one called Turbo Investments and the other one Soacha Capital."

"Much more interesting Sergeant; do go on. Does *it* own anything?"

"Well sir, it says it is an investment company and its main line of business is provision of prestige hire car services. It lists ownership of ten vehicles with a value over £1 million. Must be pretty nice cars sir."

"Indeed—is that it?"

"Not quite sir—it also owns two properties. One on the High Street at Poplar, the other on Blackwall Way at East India. It also listed business assets, stock and goodwill—that sort of thing—so I checked the businesses operating at those addresses. Both the same type ... adult shops at each location ... called Victorian Secrets. Don't know if that helps sir, but that appears to be it."

"Brilliant, Sergeant—job well done." He really had done a good job—but he had absolutely no idea what he'd uncovered. "Tell me, are you on duty this afternoon?"

"Well sir, it was to be my afternoon off. Been working quite a bit of overtime lately, weekends, that sort of thing you know. But really, I didn't have much else on anyway—just be doing a bit of shopping. What did you have in mind?"

"Off the record—would you be interested in coming with me to those shops? Just us—no-one else to know."

"I suppose so sir, fill in the day. And of course I'll say nothing—discretion is my middle name." I took that to be the sergeant's attempt at humour.

"Excellent. When you're done, why don't you grab a cab and meet me at the Landmark Hotel. Give me a call when you're approaching, and I'll meet you at the front. Don't worry about the cost—I'll pay."

"Yes sir, give me half-an-hour."

"Oh, and Sergeant, it would be very helpful if you could do two things—get search warrants for both the premises. I realise it usually takes some time, but maybe you have a quicker, *unofficial*, method available? And I know you're off-duty, but could you remain in uniform?"

I closed the phone, sat back, and smiled to myself. Talk about *non-standard procedure*! I could see the internal Yard report... *An off-duty, middle ranking officer in full uniform, and a plain clothes visiting senior officer from outside the service, today staged an unauthorised surprise search on two businesses, without the knowledge or authority of anyone in senior ranks. Further, they were armed with traditional weaponry and bogus search warrants*!

This was shaping up to be *fun*.

CHAPTER
FIFTY-SEVEN

H alf-an-hour passed; then forty-five minutes, and no call from Sergeant Shepherd. I was beginning to worry—I'd observed that while he moved slowly, no doubt due in part to his bulk, he was normally very punctual. I hoped he hadn't encountered a *problem* at the office. Thankfully my phone rang shortly after, and I made a quick beeline for the hotel entrance.

The black cab pulled up and I jumped in the back alongside the beefy sergeant. Between the two of us we certainly had it full! "Sorry I'm late—more last-minute paperwork. Something to do with *searches* I believe," he said dryly, "and I couldn't call—too many people about. Thought I should just get here as fast as I could."

"No problem," I lied, "but I was beginning to worry a bit. Now, you went to the scene where the woman was found. I'd like to go there—just so I know what we're talking about—and then to the closest of these two establishments."

"Yes sir," said the sergeant enthusiastically, warming to the task. "Driver—East India thank you—Jamestown Way."

The taxi ride was swift . . . perhaps fifteen minutes along the A501 and A13. We took the Leamouth exit, slipped through a couple of roundabouts and found ourselves in the middle of all the new high-rise development of the Docklands. A few blocks further towards the river was Jamestown Way, and at the end was a park which fronted the East India Dock Basin.

"This'll be us sir," said the sergeant. "Driver, wait here please, we'll only be five minutes."

The two of us strolled through the park and over to the edge of the Thames, gazing across the river at the Millennium Dome with all its spikes. It was thick with trees and bushes which shielded the neighbouring residential area. And forensics estimated it was after dark when the murder took place, so the location looked about perfect.

"Remind me again Sergeant, what did you *actually* find here?"

"Nothing sir, that is, no actual evidence. The body was found over there," he replied, pointing downriver towards the Trinity Buoy Wharf where about twenty assorted boats were moored. "Our best guess was she was murdered here and dumped in the water, given the state of the body and the tides at that time."

"And the residents," I asked, "nobody saw a thing?"

"No sir, except the couple who thought they heard a woman screaming, and then a bit later saw a man walking back down the street."

"Any description of him?"

"Not much—mid-sixties, seventy maybe, not too tall ... perhaps about five six or so, grey hair and wearing a flat-cap. They said he had his head down and was moving pretty fast."

Well, the description could fit Connolly if he *was* here. Then again, it could fit any one of a million men in London. I took one last look at the park as we got back in the taxi.

"Right Sergeant, this adult shop you found—let's go check out the merchandise."

CHAPTER
FIFTY-EIGHT

We pulled up about thirty yards from Victorian Secrets. Why *do* these places come up with such dreadful puns for their names I wondered? Anyway, better not to have any surveillance cameras observing us alighting from the taxi—try and retain some element of surprise!

"Please wait, and keep the motor running. We won't be long," Sarge directed the driver.

He led the way, bogus paperwork in hand. A buzzer sounded somewhere beyond us as we entered—pretty crude security I thought. I scanned the store layout—subdued lighting, a wall off to the left with about six rows of shelving, housing DVDs mostly.

Alternating shelving and glass cases in the middle, filled with cellophane wrapped magazines, dildos, vibrators and similar equipment. The rear wall contained racks of skimpy lingerie and other items of decidedly non-traditional clothing.

In the middle was a doorway with a pink sign above which read 'Private Viewing Rooms'. The wall to our right contained brightly lit shelving with all manner of sex toys and a U-shaped counter with another doorway slightly offset behind it. A long-haired man in his late-twenties sat at the counter, apparently mesmerized by something on his computer. Otherwise, the shop appeared devoid of people.

The sergeant strode up to the store attendant who was still engrossed in his computer, slapped the folded piece of paper on the counter and said briskly, "Metropolitan Police sir—we have a search warrant for these premises. Are you the manager?"

The young man slowly redirected his gaze up to the sergeant. It seemed to take a minute to register there was an actual policeman standing in front of him. "No–no I'm not the manager," he said nervously.

"Well who is, and where is he?" demanded the sergeant.

"He's out there," said the attendant indicating with his thumb the doorway behind the counter. "I'll buzz him and tell him the police are here."

"You do that laddie," said the sergeant as he started making his move towards the manager's door. The attendant grabbed the phone, pressed a button and stammered, "b–boss, the p–police are here."

Sergeant Shepherd gave two quick raps on the door, called loudly, "police—coming in," and flung the door open. While the sergeant filled the doorway side to side, I was a whole lot taller, and in a fleeting moment, I could see over his head what was now facing him.

The sergeant had taken one step into the manager's office and stopped dead in his tracks. Sitting behind his desk was the store manager with a pistol pointed directly at the sergeant. I instinctively stepped to the left out of the sightline, reached for my Glock and yelled, "Shep, down!"

The sergeant dropped to the floor; in a split second I stepped back in front of the door and away again, which was just time enough to draw the manager to fire. I stepped back into the door again and let off three quick rounds. Blood sprayed up the wall as the manager slammed backwards into it. I glanced at the young attendant, who was looking plainly terrified. "Don't you fuckin' move. Stay right where you are."

I stepped over to the sergeant who was still face-planted on the carpet. "You alright?"

"I think so—no major damage," he said, gingerly pushing himself to his knees.

I looked at the attendant, still transfixed to his chair. "Is there a safe in here?"

The attendant nodded.

"The keys—do you have them?" The attendant shook his head. "Well where are they?"

"The m–manager—he keeps them on him I think."

I stepped inside the office, gun poised, while the sergeant steadied himself and dusted off. I moved slowly around the manager's desk, just in case there was still some life left. He was splayed backwards on the floor against the wall, one arm and shoulder cocked up on it. One of my bullets had hit him directly below the left eye. I guessed that must have been the first, because there were two more bullet holes in the wall behind where he had been sitting. Either way, he was headed for the obituary notices.

CHAPTER FIFTY-NINE

I reached around his pockets pulling out bits and pieces—a wallet, handkerchief, pack of cigarettes, some gum and two sets of keys. I called out to the young attendant, "get in here."

The sergeant ushered the attendant in. He didn't know which way to look, particularly as he rounded the desk and saw his former boss with blood pooling around his shoulders. "Do you know which of these keys belongs to the safe?" I asked. The attendant fingered the keys one at a time and separated two. "One of these I think—can I go now?"

"You stay over there," I said pointing to a chair in the corner, "we'll let you know when you can go." It was then I scanned the rest of the office, and noticed piles of boxes twenty high, in a corner. I opened a couple and recognised immediately the pinkish, glass-like substance—ice ... crystal meth. I ripped open a couple of bigger boxes alongside—full of bongs. This was the Alvarez idea of a convenience store!

I took the keys and tried them on the safe, with the sergeant crouched down beside me. The second key worked and I eased the door open. Man, what a sight! The sergeant let out a long whistle. The safe, which was big enough—about six feet high and two to three feet deep—was packed with cash. Bundles and bundles of fifties—God knows how much was in there, but one thing was certain—it was way more than any adult shop would need. Proceeds from the packages, no doubt.

I slipped open a couple of drawers. Small bundles of paper grouped together, a chequebook and some rubber stamps, but nothing of obvious interest to us. I called over to the attendant again, "is there anywhere else here they keep stuff?"

He shook his head. "I don't think so."

The cash was interesting, and fitted in with the Alvarez business model, but it was not what we were looking for. Come to think of it, I didn't know what we were looking for. I knelt down, my mind running through the possibilities, and pulled out a few bundles of cash from the bottom of the stack. As I did so, I created a small cave in the pile; and that's when I noticed it . . . something white stuck underneath, and behind, the other bundles. I slid it out slowly . . . a small calico bag which was quite heavy.

"Wonder what's in here?" I asked handing the bag to the sergeant. He emptied the contents onto the desk, accompanied by another long whistle. The bag contained more cash—maybe a couple of thousand pounds—a passport in the name of Jean Gasteau, a pistol and silencer, and a navy-blue flat-cap.

"Would you take a look at that sir, items of interest I would say," said the sergeant, deadpan.

"Sergeant," I said smiling slightly, "I think we've found what we were looking for. Bag them up will you?"

I locked the safe, replaced the keys in the dead manager's pocket and ushered the attendant out to his counter. The sergeant followed, bag in hand.

"You have security cameras running in here?" I asked the attendant. He nodded. "Show me where it operates from."

He took me out through the viewing room door, to a small room off to one side. It was full of storage cupboards and recording equipment, including screens covering each of the viewing rooms. I thought to myself, "Todd, if ever you're tempted to use one of these places, there's your lesson."

The attendant showed me the recorders— one for the main store and one for the manager's office. I turned them both off and removed the drives. It also occurred to me, if Alvarez controlled this place from afar, he might want to know what happened in here *all the time*.

"The older ones—they keep copies?" I asked. He pointed to a cupboard, and I collected a box of about a dozen discs.

"I'll leave you with a number," I said to the attendant, as I headed to the shop entrance "it's the police—in a moment you can give them a call and report what happened. But you'll have to wait here—if you leave, they will think *you* did this."

I turned to the sergeant. "Right, I think that will be all here," and held up the security discs, "now let's play them at their own fucking game."

CHAPTER SIXTY

I had the taxi drop Sergeant Shepherd at his home at Tower Hamlets, which was just off the A13 on our return journey. "Bought a nice little flat there about a year ago sir—used to live further out at Enfield but it's too far. Bigger house, but it's just me and the wife now—you know how it is? Much more convenient, though I do miss the space."

I nodded sympathetically. I didn't really know 'how it is', but I was grateful we didn't have a two-hour journey somewhere, and I didn't want to just dump him on a train.

Plus, I needed some forensic work on our bag of goodies from the adult shop—fingerprints for one. But our little clandestine expedition was *highly irregular*—and that was putting it mildly. How could I then ask The Yard to examine the contents?

"Leave it with me sir, I've got someone in there, forensics that is, who can help us," the sergeant said with a wink, "and they won't say a thing either. They will just run this through with all the other washing."

It still worried me though. If we weren't careful, *we* could be charged. In fact, if they did discover that we had conducted the raid, an investigation would be a formality... just for starters! At the very least we had exceeded our authority, complete with dummy search warrants and the off-duty sergeant in full uniform. At worst... who would know?

Who was I kidding? There was no *if* they discovered... only *when*. By the time that young attendant had described us to the attending coppers, and that news got back to anyone in McClure's office, they would know exactly who had been there. That might give me till the morning. Yep, I could see the press headlines... *Scotland Yard Instigates Disciplinary Proceedings Against Two Officers.* I was going to need a good story!

"By the way Sergeant, sorry I used your nickname in there—just thought I needed your attention in a hurry."

The sergeant shook his head. "Not a problem sir, better on the floor and alive than the alternative. Shep's good any time."

I handed him a small packet from my coat. "Another video—this one from the office area of The Landmark. There's a dark Mercedes parked outside—see if your contact can make out the numberplate, could you? And if he has any luck, you might be able to trace the owner."

The sergeant nodded and grinned as he hauled himself from the taxi. "Happy to oblige—I'll call you when I have something."

The taxi dropped me back at The Landmark, and I paid the fare on my card. Thank Christ the bill was being picked up by the Australian Feds—but as I was on secondment I supposed it would end up back on McClure's desk for sign off. An hour and a half touring London doesn't come cheap.

I got back to my room and slipped the security disc from Victorian Secrets into the DVD player; I was curious to see who else might have been there before us. I made myself some tea, and settled in to watch the show.

Wham! I suddenly realised there was something else I had to do and in all the excitement in the adult shop, I'd completely forgotten. Watch the video footage by all means, but then I'd better prepare. I had a *dinner date with Cindy.*

CHAPTER
SIXTY-ONE

The early footage from the store contained nothing. Only a few customers and quite frankly, their interests and mine appeared substantially different. I showered and changed, grabbed a bottle from the room bar—a Cirrus Syrah 2007 which meant little to me, but in moments like this I had to trust the management's wine knowledge—then headed down to the lobby for a cab to Covent Garden.

Again I had the driver drop me some distance from Cindy's apartment. It appeared that everywhere I went, someone else always seemed to know I was there. I didn't feel that I was being followed—then again, maybe I was. But somehow, someone was tracking me. Still,

I enjoyed walking around her neighbour-hood—it reminded me a lot of the more vibrant parts of Sydney at night. Woolloomooloo maybe? God, it seemed a life-time since I was home.

I pressed the buzzer on her intercom; smack on seven. This time she answered. "Come in honey, on time as always."

I took the lift up to the second floor, where she was waiting for me at her open door. She was dressed in a loose white t-shirt, light blue body-hugging jeans and a loosely knotted scarf of the same colour. And bare feet. She looked *fabulous*! I hugged her and planted a kiss where it mattered most.

She had a bottle of white wine open so I joined her in some, sitting myself at her breakfast bar and making light chit-chat, while she attended to dinner preparations. I took in the apartment—new, or newly refurb'ed anyway, a couple of bedrooms and big windows that overlooked the street and old buildings opposite. Very stylish! All in all, it was a pretty impressive pad for someone on a PA's salary.

Dinner came—mussels in white wine, the juiciest pork chops in Marsala I have ever eaten, and the creamiest ice cream covered in frozen berries. Oh, and my bottle of red, of course. Not only was she beautiful and a great lover, the girl could cook! Dinner over and lights dimmed, we settled into her plush sofa with a bottle of port, her head resting on my shoulder, and Norah Jones lilting quietly in the background.

"How's your hunting going," she asked referring to my ongoing investigation, "any progress?"

"Some leads, a bit of new information here and there. What about McClure—is he getting anywhere?"

Cindy shrugged. "Don't know—he doesn't tell me much, and we've had no more meetings since you were in."

"Strange," I said reflectively, "he seems to have gone quiet on it. Lost interest or something. Anyway, I didn't come here to talk shop." I kissed her gently on the top of her head.

She cocked her head and looked up at me. "Feel like a little activity to settle dinner?" she asked cheekily, nodding towards the bedroom.

"I thought you'd never ask," I said, hauling her up from the sofa. Arms around each other we made for the boudoir. My phone blurted, which made her jump slightly. "Sorry, better take this," I said glancing at the screen.

It was Sergeant Shepherd.

"Sorry to disturb you sir, but I didn't want to let things rest. Delivered those items to my colleague later this afternoon, and he's just come to see me on his way home with the results. Is now a good time?"

I turned away from Cindy and moved towards the living room windows. "Fine—go ahead."

"Fingerprints sir; on the banknotes too hard, too many, but on the gun and silencer some belonging to our Mr Connolly."

"Very good," I said, trying not to sound too excited.

"And the hat sir, a couple of hairs found in it. They were a DNA match also for Connolly. His records are on file from his prison stint sir."

"Just what we were looking for—good work and thank you for your help. I can't talk much now . . ."

"I realise that sir, but two more things of importance. Prints also found on the gun and silencer... belonging to Juanita Sanchez. Ballistics report matches it as the weapon *which killed all three.* I have retrieved the items sir, and have them stored securely. And lastly, the Mercedes car is registered to Providencia Investment."

There was total silence for ten seconds. It felt like ten minutes. "I understand. Thank you very much again—I'll call you tomorrow." I closed off the call.

Holy shit! We had the evidence to nail Connolly. My mind was flying—thoughts coming a thousand a second, and I was trying to process it all at once. Did he kill *all three*? Why were Sanchez's prints on the gun? There was no way now I could make love to Cindy with my head in this state. I *had* to get out of there.

"Who was it—is everything alright?" she asked, looking concerned.

"Darling," and I put my arms around her, my mind searching for the gentlest white lie I could think of, "I'm so sorry, but that was a call from the US. Thank you so much for a fabulous dinner but I *have* to go."

"Oh... Oh, do you have to—anyone I know, maybe I can help?"

"No, I don't think so—I'll have to do this myself," I said as I opened the door, "it involves Connolly. I need to pay him another visit—now."

I kissed her fully on the lips. But in that moment for the first time, the beautiful serenity had vanished; her body seemed taut, frigid even, and her face had formed a *definite scowl.*

CHAPTER SIXTY-TWO

I got to the street outside Cindy's flat, and for some reason I was gasping for air. Goodness knows why—I hadn't done anything physical—must have been the stress of having to deal with the sergeant's call, and get away from Cindy to clear my head. To think only moments before we were on our way to bed! No wonder she didn't look pleased.

I needed to get back to the hotel—plans to make. I joined the throng of tourists generally moving to and fro through Covent Garden, but this time I was *not* going to walk—there was no telling who might be tailing me. I headed for the tube station as fast as I could, and found a taxi lurking nearby, trolling for a fare.

Back at the hotel I booked a flight from Heathrow for early in the morning to Toulon, with a return the following day. It was impossible at short notice to get direct flights, so I had to make do with a stopover. At this stage it was 'whatever it takes'—I felt, no, *I knew*, I had to get to Connolly.

I then rang the sergeant. "Shep, sorry to call you so late but I couldn't really talk earlier. Great work on the evidence, and I'm heading to see if I can get to Connolly first thing in the morning. I'm worried though that The Yard might get onto us and our little visit today. If they ask you—deny everything! Know nothing! They don't *know* it was us— and we've got the videos. I'll call you when I get back."

"No problem sir, hope it goes well. I'll be careful—had a lovely time shopping on my afternoon off, if you get my drift?"

I settled in to watch the security videos from the adult shop. Damn boring stuff, and after a couple of hours I floated off to sleep. The alarm snapped me back to life at four-thirty the next morning, I packed my bags—

everything—and checked out of The Landmark.

At Heathrow I put my belongings into the 'left luggage' storage—thought I'd take a chance on the clothes I was wearing lasting the distance—and by seven-thirty I was in the air, en route to Toulon.

CHAPTER
SIXTY-THREE

P lease repeat what you have just told me," said Ernesto Alvarez tersely into the telephone. His lawyer was on the line with news of a police search at one of the company businesses, Victorian Secrets at East India. Given the director, Juanita Sanchez, was dead, the investigating police did not know who else to contact. So they had rung the registered office, which happened to be that of the Alvarez legal team.

"Two policemen, one in uniform the other plainclothes, conducted a search of the premises. They had a warrant apparently. It appears the manager pulled a gun on them, and they shot him. He is dead. The young store attendant is okay, and he called the police," the lawyer advised matter-of-factly.

"What God damn policemen, what were their names? When did this happen?" Alvarez demanded.

"The incident took place this afternoon. The police who rang had no background on the search warrant, so they don't know the identity of the policemen. It was early in their investigation, they said; they have the shop now sealed off as a crime scene and the attendant has been questioned and sent home. They will let us know when you can have access again to the premises," the lawyer continued.

"Did they say anything else—has anything been taken, broken into, what were they looking for? Any... damage?" Alvarez was becoming more agitated.

"Apparently no damage. Everything appeared in order, except of course for the dead manager. Oh, yes, the attendant did say they opened the safe and took a bag from it, but that was all."

"Shit," snapped Alvarez, "that's it?"

"I believe so—oh, and they took the security discs as well."

There was a long silence as Alvarez gazed out across the dazzling lights of London, processing *this* piece of news. "I'm going down there—see what else I can find."

"But Mr Alvarez, you can't go in—it's late and the police have it sealed off."

"Fuck the police. Don't you worry—I'll handle it." Alvarez hung up the phone, and thought momentarily. Who would mount a raid on one of his establishments? Why didn't he know—he *always* received a call if something like this was about to happen? Now he had police, *unknown* police, crawling all over the shop. And all that inventory, and evidence ... totally at risk!

Still, he couldn't be seen to have any connection to the business. If anybody associated him with it, particularly if they now knew what was inside, it would put all his other similar operations at risk. But he couldn't bear the thought of *not* knowing—not being able to see with his own eyes.

"John," he called to his driver and orderly, "ready the car, will you? I want to go to East India." The driver disappeared in the express lift to the basement, and Alvarez reached for his overcoat.

The telephone rang as he was about to enter the lift. "Damn," he muttered as he retraced his steps to answer it. "Yes?" he snapped.

The familiar voice came on the line, with no introduction or greeting. "Have you heard the news?"

"Of course, the lawyer has just told me about the raid."

"Don't know about any raid—what I'm calling about is Todd."

"What about *him*?" Alvarez spat. The mere mention of his name was agitating.

"He's on his way to see Connolly. Tomorrow."

It immediately dawned on Alvarez who might be behind this raid. And now he was armed with evidence, direct from the safe, and on camera.

"Bastard!" swore Alvarez, "this prick is *bad* for business. This has *got to stop*!"

CHAPTER
SIXTY-FOUR

The flight with stopover took some time and it was mid-afternoon when I finally arrived at Hyeres airport. I took a taxi around to Sanary-Sur-Mer and settled in at a cafe on the waterfront. The sight of the hotel at the end of the quay stirred the memory of that wonderful night of passion with Cindy a couple of weeks ago. So much had happened in the interim, it felt like a different lifetime.

I was in no hurry to move; I planned to drop in on Connolly as dark approached, and a little after six I took another taxi and headed down the peninsula, following the Mediterranean, past the yacht club and finally onto

Connolly's street. The water looked sublime—grey and peaceful—in the fading light.

I assumed he would have security cameras everywhere, so I had the taxi drop me about a hundred yards from the villa. Same approach this time... I moved as quickly and quietly as possible down the long private drive, using the trees and bushes as camouflage. The villa's tall, ornate, double-entrance gates were locked. A little further on was a single access gate which I scaled, and dropped in quietly alongside the house.

I crept around the front, to the large terrace overlooking the water, and could make out a couple of big cane armchairs. A balding head protruded above one, facing out over the grey sea. I moved quickly on to the terrace drawing my Glock as I got closer. *How would he react?* I had to be prepared.

"Paul Connolly," I said briskly and the diminutive figure suddenly moved, struggling to his feet.

He stood facing me, processing the scene. *"You,"* he yelled, "what the fuck are *you* doing here?"

"I've come to arrest you—for the murder of Andrew Lau, Terry Walker and Juanita Sanchez."

"Like *hell* you have! You can't arrest me. I've killed no-one—and you have no proof," he scoffed.

"I have plenty of proof—more than you can imagine, and I *can* arrest you . . . ."

"*What* proof do you have?" he demanded, cutting in.

"That's confidential; but believe me I've got it. So unless you have a very good reason for me not to take you in, you can look forward to rotting away your life in Wandsworth again."

Connolly put his head down, staring at the terrace floor, and shaking it every few seconds. He seemed to be murmuring "no, no" to himself, as if in some kind of trance. Finally he looked up at me, the bluff and bluster now totally gone.

"I can't go back to the slammer. A long, slow death like that would be unbearable. I'd rather d–die now. If I tell you what I know, can we do a deal? That is . . . you leave me alone for good."

"Depends what you tell me—what sort of information have you got?"

"I'll tell you what I know . . . about Perez, and the Alvarez empire; the money trail and all that sort of thing. His other businesses—I know nothing about them. But if I tell you all about the money, do we have a deal?"

I thought for a moment. He looked suddenly so pathetic, so vulnerable, and I started to feel sorry for him. Hell, I thought, he's an old man, and on his own he's a threat to nobody. It's the bigger fish I was really after—Alvarez and his cronies. Still, I did have his prints on a murder weapon.

"Right, you tell me what you know. If it's enough, if the information is useful and not just meandering bullshit, I'll leave you alone. For good! But it's up to you." The terrace was now in darkness, but the villa was lit up inside as if for a party. I indicated for him to sit down, and I eased myself into the second armchair.

"Okay Mr Connolly," I said fixing my gaze on him, "start talking."

CHAPTER
SIXTY-FIVE

Connolly began by going over a lot of old ground, stuff I already knew from his previous case and from my conversations with Tommy Garcia and David Perez. How he was recruited by Perez as the front man for Calima Ministries, offering loans for major property deals, and how the money never arrived. He then began to expand on the money source, which I found much more interesting.

"Of course," Connolly continued, "we knew where the money was coming from. Or more correctly, we assumed we knew where it was from. It was drug proceeds, and they needed a way to legitimise it. Just a classic laundering operation—we lent the money out to legitimate borrowers for major property deals, and when it was repaid, it was clean."

"So it was Alvarez money behind it all?" I asked.

"Yes—or really it was Rodriguez money. He was the main supplier for Alvarez as far as I know, but as I said, I had nothing to do with that stuff. Anyway, they never came through with it. Put us *right* in the shit—me anyway."

"Yeah, you took the fall for them."

Connolly's head dropped again at the thought. "I blame the boys. You know, Rodriguez was an old man and his two sons were taking over more and more of their business. Well, that was according to David Perez. Anyway, I think they got cold feet—the old man had some arrangement with Alvarez, we went out and secured the deals, then they pulled the plug. Left us hanging out to dry."

"And your clients weren't happy?" I said, trying to show some sympathy for him.

"Not fucking happy! You kidding? They came after us, lawyers blazing. Alvarez told me that if I said nothing, and took the hit for them, he would look after me. Which I did— five years in that bastard of a place, and *you* put me there. Anyway, he was as good as his word. He owns all this," said Connolly turning slightly and sweeping his arm in an arc across the front of the villa, "and I'm a kept man, though occasionally he extracts a piece of my flesh."

"Which brings us to now," I said, "so what about Andrew Lau; what's he got to do with Alvarez, and why did you kill him?"

"I *didn't* damn well kill him," Connolly spat. "I don't know what arrangement he had with Alvarez. Lau rang here one day—tracked me down sometime after I was released. Wanted to know if I was back in the game— the big money and all that. I told him I wasn't, but I mentioned it to Alvarez and he asked me to set up a meeting. I did, and left it at that."

"Well they must have had some disagreement, because it has cost Lau his life. And as I said—we've got the evidence."

"If you want my take on it—Lau was a smart man. Wealthy, cashed up, with an international business and he was set up to trade all-round the globe. He was always after another good deal, as long as it was big. Perfect fit for Alvarez. He needs that sort of player to channel some of his operation through."

"You mean launder his dirty proceeds; but why have him killed?"

"Don't know—as I said I was not part of it—but I would put it down to one thing—greed. That's usually behind most of these things, isn't it? You're the bloody detective!" he said sarcastically.

I let the remark slide. "Well, what about Walker? Why was he involved?"

"I think he and Lau kept in touch. Walker was always a much smaller player but they got on—at least they did when I dealt with them. Maybe Walker was trying to do deals with Lau. Lau had the money, and people like Walker will always hang round trying to get some rub-off."

I was getting a clearer picture of how things had transpired. Maybe! True, I still didn't know why Lau had been killed, but if he was going to run some money laundering for Alvarez, the possibilities were endless. However, I still had no background on these murders.

"And Juanita Sanchez... what was her involvement with Alvarez that would get her killed, that would require you to bump her off?"

Connolly ignored the last question. "I don't know much of her background," he lied, "but I do know that she and Alvarez were quite often an item."

I raised a questioning eyebrow. In the half-dark he must have seen the incredulous look on my face.

"That's right," said Connolly, "Alvarez was shagging Sanchez."

"Amazing," I said, spluttering slightly, "and to think she's Perez . . ."

At that moment the door chimes rang at the front of the villa. "Who in the hell could that be?" muttered Connolly, as he rose to answer it.

I sat for a couple of seconds, and a very uneasy feeling came over me. Weren't the front gates locked? So how did someone get to the front door, and why? Only uninvited guests, like me, came over the side gate. I left my chair and headed back around the house the way I had entered.

As I neared the front of the house I could see two men standing at the front door. I heard the door open and Connolly say "Oh, it's you..." There was a muffled 'pop, pop'. If I wasn't mistaken, that was the sound of gun-shots, with silencer. Time to leave!

I clambered back over the access gate, which rattled slightly as I jumped off. I crept quickly back past the entrance gates, and could see the lifeless body of Connolly in his doorway. Dead? Looked like it! The two assailants had obviously heard the gate rattle, and were now slowly advancing toward the main gates... toward *me*... guns drawn. I bolted up the drive.

I kept as close to the shrubbery as possible and didn't look back, but I could hear the automatic gates open. Then more 'pops'—three or four in quick succession—and a bullet smacked into a tree near my head. I ran as hard as I could out on to the street, but which way now? Then I remembered when Connolly had rammed our car and taken off—Cindy couldn't see him for the trees—so I headed in the same direction.

I weaved slowly through the bush, branches catching my clothes, tearing at my skin. A car approached, parking lights on, the occupants flashing a torch from side to side, searching. I crouched low in the undergrowth hoping they couldn't hear my frantic breathing, and thankfully watched the taillights recede. I decided to walk back to the town, keeping to backstreets as much as possible. With every approaching vehicle I hid, and waited, and waited, until I was sure it had gone.

After nearly two hours of painful progress, I arrived back at the waterfront. The Hotel de la Tour sign loomed large . . . it looked like just the type of respite I needed. The owner looked up at me with a slightly amazed expression, no doubt due to my dishevelled state. Then a big smile lit his face.

"Ah, the policeman from Australia—welcome back. And your lovely wife—she is with you, yes?"

"Unfortunately, no—just me this time. Would you have a vacancy?"

"Of course, of course—I will put you in the same one you had before," he said handing me the key. "Anything you need, just call."

I was never more pleased to reach the sanctuary of my room. I gazed out over the harbour, the moon reflecting off the black water and illuminating the moored boats. Well, at least I was in a better place than

Connolly. Or maybe not. Maybe he had his wish.

After all, he did tell me he'd *rather die now*.

CHAPTER
SIXTY-SIX

I caught my return flight to Heathrow the following day. It was a repeat of the trip to Toulon, and again was mid-afternoon when I touched down. I'd been going over the events of the previous twenty-four hours, but it seemed to me that while I occasionally made some progress, each time I met with a 'person of interest' I came away with more questions than answers.

I believed Connolly had indeed killed Juanita Sanchez. His prints were on the weapon and a man matching his description was seen leaving the area shortly afterward. We had the method, we had the hard evidence, but the motive? My guess... after

listening to Connolly's version of history...
was that he was *directed* to kill her.

What was it he had said—that he was a
"kept man", but sometimes had to contribute
a piece of "his flesh"? I figured that was the
price of being 'kept'—sometimes he had to do
little jobs for the boss, contribute something
to the cause. Like killing Juanita Sanchez!

Not that it mattered much now—I
assumed Connolly was dead. No doubt someone in the food chain would get word of it, and
let me know. But who would want to kill him?
Alvarez? Maybe, but why—Connolly was
keeping his nose clean? He didn't seem to
have other enemies—outside the immediate
Alvarez clan he appeared to have little contact
with anyone.

Except now, of course. *With me*!

And that was the other thing—there was
this rising tide of uneasiness within me that
wherever I went, trouble seemed to follow. In
fact, it often seemed to get there before me, and
sooner or later I was going to be caught out.

The law of averages says that if you keep
getting belted, tortured, run down, and shot
at, eventually one of them is going to find its
mark. And that could be *terminal*.

Maybe it was just coincidence, but who-ever did not want me around always seemed to know my movements. Their information was obviously good, but where it came from I didn't know—there were always a couple of possibilities—but I made a mental note to start taking a more active interest; try and detect a pattern.

I retrieved my luggage from storage at Heathrow, and headed back to The Landmark where I'd rebooked. With Connolly presuma-bly now gone, I could get back to the main game, the original reason I came here—to help find the killer, or killers, of Andrew Lau and Terry Walker.

That was *it*, I decided, my *focus* from here on in. Review the evidence I had, including the security discs from the adult shop, and what evidence I was missing. Focus on who might want to stop me, and why. Lastly, look hard at likely motives of those involved. That would give me something to occupy my mind. Trouble was . . . at times my definite course of action went the way I planned, and at other times it bore absolutely no resemblance.

Funny isn't it, the thoughts that come to mind? I found myself back in the hotel room, security footage playing, and I couldn't get Connolly out of my head. The original case, the time he spent in prison, and his outwardly affluent life since. But it wasn't affluent—that was just a façade—because in a sense he was still in prison, albeit a comfortable one. House arrest, I guess.

Sure he could be obnoxious and arrogant, but they were really just a defence. And he was certainly delusional. Now he was gone—no family, no friends, or none who were around—just a lonely old man, who, somewhere along his journey, had got way out of his depth.

CHAPTER SIXTY-SEVEN

I sat for hours glued to the television, the security footage rolling on and on. I didn't know what else to do—I had no more evidence so this seemed to be the most productive option. At least it filled in time until I could sleep. One o'clock came and went, as did two; more of the same nondescript stuff—the odd customer poring over videos and magazines, an occasional visitor to the viewing rooms. Then two men entered the shop, and even in my semi-awake state, that jolted me back to the present.

The first was big, solidly built, wearing a suit and gloves. Gloves? If I wasn't mistaken that was the same man caught on the security tape at The Landmark... the driver of the dark Mercedes. This time though, he had a companion. An older man, grey-haired and perhaps nearing seventy. Trouble was, his back was to the camera and I just couldn't get a fix on his face.

Both men entered the manager's office and I took a note of the time on the footage—twelve-fifteen the day prior to our little surprise visit. I flipped through the remaining security discs which were colour-coded, and grouped them accordingly. I needed one covering the manager's office at that time.

I played quick bites from each and finally located the disc for the correct day, which I fast forwarded to the appropriate time. Right on cue, our two visitors from the front counter walked in. They greeted the manager without any fuss—more a nod of the head from each—and strode directly to the pile of boxes in the corner. The driver opened some of each; the older man pulled a few packets of meth out which he held up for inspection, and then replaced them.

Meanwhile the manager had taken some bundles of cash from the safe, and piled them on his desk. Assuming one thousand pounds per bundle, I guessed there was about thirty thousand sitting there. This he collected together, and placed in a calico bag. The driver then gathered four boxes of ice, and two of bongs, which he separated out into a neat pile in the front corner of the office. The manager placed the bag of cash on top.

Their task complete, the two visitors nodded again to the manager, and the older man appeared to give some instruction. Finally, both men turned to leave and were facing the camera. I had never met him, but I was absolutely *certain* the older man was Ernesto Alvarez. *Caught*—handling the merchandise! That was all I needed.

First thing in the morning I was going to call Detective Chief Inspector McClure. He *needed* to see this.

CHAPTER
SIXTY-EIGHT

Despite my lack of sleep, I woke early, about six. I was excited at having some evidence which put Alvarez directly at the coalface—handling illegal drugs. And he was clearly in control, directing his manager and his driver. It wasn't enough to get him for murder, but it was a start. At eight o'clock, I called McClure on his mobile.

"Good news," I said excitedly, "I've got something you ought to see."

"What, what have you got?" he said, but I noted he didn't seem to share my excitement. Maybe even a touch nervous.

"Evidence—not precisely what I was looking for, but evidence nonetheless. Either way, I think you will want to see it."

"What sort of evidence? Do you want to bring it in?" I was a bit concerned again at the inspector's lack of enthusiasm; his apparent caution.

"No—easier if you come here. I'm at The Landmark, so let's say about twelve and you give me a call when you get here," I replied, trying to seize the initiative. He agreed with the plan and signed off.

The more I thought about the upcoming meeting, the more uneasy I felt. I rang down to reception. "Good morning Commander," answered the male receptionist, "this is Charles—how can I help?"

"Just the man I wanted. Charles, I need you to do something for me... could you come to the room as soon as possible? But just you."

"Be there in five minutes sir," he said brightly.

Charles rapped on the door shortly afterward and I ushered him into the room. I showed him the set of security discs and asked if he could copy them. I explained again that this should remain under the radar . . . that he should tell no-one. Also, that I needed a particular disc back, fast.

"Not a word sir, but it will take some time, and I have to attend to my official duties you understand. Still, I'll have the VIP disc done within the hour," he said as he let himself out the door.

I showered and dressed, then called room service to deliver breakfast. As promised, Charles returned with the first disc, saying he was due to finish at two, but thought he would have all the copies done by then. He really seemed to enjoy helping—I guessed most young people, seeing it from the outside, thought amateur sleuthing was a bit of fun. Whatever it was, I was grateful for his interest.

A little before twelve McClure called saying he was about five minutes away. I slipped down to the lobby in time to see the DCI's limo pull up out front, and the inspector make his way into the hotel. Thankfully he was alone. We shook hands and headed up to my room.

"Well, Ash, what's with all the hush-hush ... this vital evidence?" he asked, smiling slightly.

"Something I want you to see," I replied, pressing the remote-control of the DVD player. I had the disc set to begin at the precise time the two men entered the manager's office, and let it play until they had walked out of the room. The DCI watched in silence—stony silence—and then turned to me.

"Where did you get this?" he asked, smiling no longer. "Is this it, or is there something more?"

"It was delivered to me on its own—no sender details. And from what I can see, that's a decent size drug supply. Crystal meth at a guess." That was a lie ... there was no guess about it. But the last thing I needed anyone to *know* was that I had been part of that raid. They could think, or assume, whatever they liked, but I was damned if I was going to tell them.

"But Jim, what I want you to confirm for me," I continued, "is the older man—the one giving orders and handling the pile of drugs— I don't know him, but to me that man is Alvarez. You've seen enough of him to know."

McClure replayed the last portion of disc, apparently studying the two figures in great detail. Finally he looked up.

"You know Ash, I think you may be right. It certainly could be him. It's a lucky break to get this sort of evidence, but I need to make sure. Okay if I take it with me?"

"Sure, take it. Doesn't seem to be much else on there—only the office person in and out, going about his work. But it will be good to have it confirmed. Interesting, isn't it, that little pile of drugs and cash they set aside—wonder what that was about?"

McClure stood abruptly and removed the DVD, slipping it inside his uniform coat.

"Who would know," he said somewhat sternly, "but I'll have it checked out." He held out his hand and we shook, but he looked decidedly unhappy.

I, however, was happy. I had a copy of that disc.

CHAPTER
SIXTY-NINE

I spent the next few hours, locked in my hotel room, reviewing the additional security discs from the adult shop—alternating between footage from the main shop and the manager's office to relieve the boredom. I was really looking forward to hearing back from McClure, to get confirmation on whether it really was Alvarez handling the drugs. I expected it shouldn't take too long—somebody in the Met should be able to ID him in an instant.

About two-thirty the hotel phone buzzed. Might be McClure, I thought—not many people knew where I was staying. I picked up the receiver and was surprised to hear Charles, the duty manager, on the line.

"Commander, I have the other items you requested—is it convenient for me to deliver them now?" I assured him it was. "Also, I have someone else I'd like you to talk to—will that be okay?"

I was intrigued. Why would a young duty manager, conducting a confidential, off-the-record assignment, want to involve somebody else?

"Sure," I said, "bring them along."

I pulled my Glock from its holster, and sat it on the table nearby. I trusted Charles, but the way this was heading there was no point taking a chance. He may have been spotted, and our whole little operation compromised.

Shortly afterward there was a rap on the door, which I opened slowly with a firm grip on my pistol. Charles stood there holding a small package, and I indicated to him to come in.

"And your friend?" I asked, raising an eyebrow.

Charles hesitated, then called back down the hallway, "come on, hurry."

In a moment another young man appeared in my doorway. I did a double-take as the second duty manager—the one who'd given hotel security footage to the Alvarez driver—scurried into the room. Of all people, why in the hell would Charles involve *him* in what I was doing? I indicated for both of them to sit down.

I looked at Charles. "This better be good."

"The discs ... original and copies," said Charles solemnly, handing me the parcel he had been holding. "Commander, this is Ryan. He is also a duty manager here and you've seen him—on the security footage—I'm sure you remember."

"I do ... and he knows what is on these discs?"

"Yes—Ryan came in early for a change of shift today. I–I'm afraid I haven't been totally honest with you."

I fixed him with my most serious stare. "Go on."

"You see," continued Charles, "a few days ago, after you checked out, I found Ryan retrieving another parcel from the hotel safe. He had finished his shift and was about to leave, so I asked him what he was taking." Charles paused momentarily and glanced at Ryan, then took a deep breath. "He'd made copies, just like I did today, of the security

338 | Ross Crothers

footage he'd given to the driver—the ones they came to collect."

I looked over at Ryan. "You still have them?"

Ryan nodded a couple of times. "After the murders of the two men, I was asked to retrieve the footage and store it in the safe. It sat there for several days, then someone rang and told me they would collect it that evening; they asked what time I finished my shift and said for me to meet them at the back door as I was leaving."

"I see, and that's the footage Charles copied for me, showing you meeting with them. So you kept a copy of what you handed over—smart thinking."

"For insurance sir," said Ryan, "the voice on the line could have been anybody—and the camera clearly showed two people going to the room where the murder took place, not long before. It also caught the same people coming into the hotel, and leaving together. I didn't want to be implicated in any way, so I thought I should keep a copy."

"Good work," I said, "but what were you doing removing the copies—when Charles spotted you?"

"You recall the footage of my meeting the driver, and as I left the hotel to go home I spoke to someone in the car. A Mercedes I think it was."

I nodded.

"Well that man promised me that if I kept my mouth shut, he would send me money in a few days. Five hundred pounds he said. That was more than two weeks ago, and no money. For my own protection I decided to get the evidence out of there."

"You weren't thinking blackmail, were you?"

"No," said Ryan, "only if anybody else found them, and it got back to the man in the car, I could be in shit. He was obviously not a man of his word . . . you know, like, where's the money? So I thought I should store them elsewhere. They might be handy later."

"Okay," I said, "so Charles knows you've got the copies. How does that put you here, now, in this room? For what purpose?"

"Charles said that I should be very careful dealing with those men. He said if anything else happened with them, then I should tell him. I didn't know what he knew about them, or why I should tell him, but he told me to keep it quiet and that he was helping you." Ryan dropped his gaze. "You know, that you were here working on the murders."

I shot a glance at Charles, who was also now looking at the floor. Anywhere but at *me*.

"Normally Charles, I'd be mad as hell that you mentioned this. You were to keep this quiet. However, in the circumstances, you've done a bloody good job. But I still don't know why Ryan is here—he has the copies and you think I'd like them—is that it?"

Charles and Ryan looked at each other, before Ryan resumed. "No sir, well, maybe . . . but not exactly. As Charles said I came in early today. I walked out behind the concierge desk before starting my shift, and that's when I saw him."

"Saw who?"

"The man who had spoken to me in the car," Ryan continued, "the one who promised me the money. And then I realised he was the same one who asked me to put the original footage in the safe. So when I saw Charles, I told him that I'd seen him. That's why I'm now here."

"So, tell me," I said looking at both, "who is this mysterious man?"

"You had a visitor about midday sir, someone from Scotland Yard I believe," said Ryan.

I nodded.

"That's the man sir—*he's the one* who took the security videos and promised me the money."

CHAPTER
SEVENTY

I was dumbstruck. This couldn't be.

This young man sitting in front of me—a twenty-something hotel duty manager—had just identified, no accused, one of the most senior officers in Scotland Yard as directly involved in tampering with evidence relating to a double murder. And offering money—a bribe?

Detective Chief Inspector James McClure was a friend of mine. A professional friendship more than social, sure, but we had known each other for over ten years. I thought I knew him well! His reputation in the force was exemplary. He was a mentor to so many junior officers, and at every opportunity held up as a model policeman. For God's sake ... Jim

McClure was what every young detective aspired to be. Surely he could not have stooped to this level? There *must* be some explanation.

I thanked Charles and Ryan for the information, and they left with Ryan promising to deliver his security copies to me immediately. Like a hot Christmas dinner in a one-hundred-degree Aussie summer, this just didn't make sense. Why would McClure get *me* to come and help investigate if he didn't want the damn thing solved? Why not give it to one of his underlings—someone he could control? Then again, why would he *not* want it solved?

I had to concede though, Ryan was probably on the money. He was young, and young eyes and ears don't play tricks the way older ones do. Anyway, the footage would confirm something—who was in the room at the time of the murder. And there was no doubt I had a strong feeling The Yard had slowed up on the investigation. Indeed as I thought about it, I found myself wondering if McClure had deliberately chosen not to investigate certain things. Things that I had suggested—like the ownership of businesses around where Juanita Sanchez was killed.

Ryan was back in fifteen minutes, package of discs in hand. He said nothing as I opened the door, merely extending the article to me. I motioned for him to come in.

"Ryan, if what we have here is as you've indicated, then you are dealing with some damned dangerous people. If the Scotland Yard inspector is also involved, then it raises additional complications. I'm talking about *your life*. What time do you finish tonight?"

"Midnight—all being well."

"Then come back here before you leave— I'll look at what you've given me in the meantime."

I opened the package; there were two discs each identified with red felt tip marker—one marked 'foyer' and the other 'corridor'. I slotted the first disc, pressed play, and watched perhaps four or five minutes of footage showing the coming and going of hotel guests, delivery people and others, through reception. Then a balding, grey-haired man in a longish, black coat entered the hotel and walked to the check-in counter. On his arm was an attractive woman, long dark hair and about early-forties, who was smartly dressed in a cream pants suit.

The couple spoke momentarily to the receptionist, signed some paperwork, and turned for the lifts. Now they were facing the camera and there was no doubt—the man appeared identical to the one caught on camera in the adult shop. The same one who's ID I was still waiting for McClure to confirm . . . who I believed was Alvarez. But the woman— that was easy. I'd seen so many photographs of her when I first began this case—the woman was definitely Juanita Sanchez.

After the couple entered the lift the disc went blank for fifteen or twenty seconds. It then resumed with them exiting the lift, and heading for the hotel entrance. Their backs were to the camera, but if I wasn't mistaken they seemed to be moving somewhat faster leaving, than they were arriving! The footage was dated and I noted that about fifty-five minutes had elapsed between the two trips in the lift. The disc then went blank again, so I assumed Ryan had copied only the relevant sections covering their arrival and departure.

I changed discs and began watching the one marked 'corridor'. It was deathly boring— it ran for more than twenty minutes showing mostly vacant hallway, with an occasional staff member hurrying through. It did, however show the couple—Alvarez and Sanchez—walking from the lift and entering a room on the left, a little over half way down. I assumed that would be 460, but that would be easy enough to check. It also showed the couple making their way back to the lift, just before the end.

Of most interest, the footage captured two men. It had been many years since I last saw them, and their backs were mostly to the camera, but there was a clear view just as they entered the room. There was no doubt the two men were Andrew Lau and Terry Walker. They entered Room 460 four minutes before the end of footage. They came out *in body bags*!

No wonder Alvarez wanted *this* removed from circulation. Short of being caught in the act, they were about as incriminating as you get. Of course, I had my other evidence in hand—I had the weapon used to murder Walker and Lau, complete with Sanchez fingerprints. She was in the room at the time of death so it now seemed pretty obvious—Juanita Sanchez was our murderer. But there was no way she was the driving force in this, and it was a moot point—she was dead too, so no advantage chasing that line of enquiry further.

What was it the forensics had uncovered? Someone had sex in that room. From DNA recovered they knew one was Sanchez, but the male partner was unknown. Connolly had told me Alvarez and Sanchez were an item so I made a mental note—when I got to Alvarez, whenever that might be, get his DNA.

What a charming piece he was, I thought. Getting one away with his sometime girl-friend, before instructing her to blow out the brains of two men. What was worse, one of those men was her live-in lover! And as a final thank you for 'services rendered,' have her eliminated and sent for fish food. *Absolutely charming*!

CHAPTER
SEVENTY-ONE

I was working through the ramifications of all this, trying to figure out McClure's *real* involvement. How would I approach him? What if he was doing actual police work... that he really *was* behind the scenes trying to catch a killer? Then I realised I had a whole lot more evidence to review—more footage from the adult shop. I fired up the DVD yet again, and settled back.

Afternoon became evening, then dark. I rang room service and ordered dinner, and the action, or more precisely, lack of it, rolled on and on. I switched back and forth between shopfront and manager's office; nothing unusual. Room service arrived and I settled in to dine, half-watching the television screen. Something caught my eye.

Somebody different had entered the manager's office; not the store attendant, and definitely not Alvarez or his driver. His back was to the camera and I couldn't make him out; he was dressed casually in denims, spray jacket and baseball cap, but the rear profile looked familiar. I fast-forwarded but he remained firmly facing away, talking to the manager. He moved out of view, perhaps back into the main store. I swapped discs, and he appeared talking to the young attendant, but *still* with his back to camera.

Why hadn't I picked him up entering the shop earlier? I was about to rewind, but he disappeared again, presumably back to the manager's office. I swapped discs *again* and sure enough, there he was in conversation with the manager. He pulled a small package from inside his coat, handed it over and pointed in the direction of the front corner of the office. He then moved over to the pile of crystal meth and cash, placed there earlier by Alvarez and his driver.

He bent down to pick up the bounty, turning to the camera as he counted the cash;

replaced the notes in the calico bag, and slipped it inside his jacket with a reassuring pat. I sat open-mouthed. This changed everything!

Standing there in full view for the world to see, pocketing £30,000 in drug proceeds and Lord knows what quantity of ice, was Detective Chief Inspector James McClure.

CHAPTER SEVENTY-TWO

I had no idea how I was going to handle this—how would I broach the subject for a start. I had immense respect for Jim McClure, and I didn't want to offend him ... but offence now appeared to be the least of his concerns. Avoiding a long jail stint might become his top priority.

Ryan, the young duty manager, tapped on my door shortly after midnight. "Take a day off," I told him, "or maybe two—call in sick. This looks dangerous, so stay away until I ring you—and don't talk to anyone. Understood?" He nodded and said nothing, as he slipped off quickly towards the lift.

I slept fitfully and woke about eight, but felt I'd been up half the night. I showered and poked at my room service breakfast, trying to work out a game-plan for the morning. Where to start? I could hardly ring and say, "hi Jim, hope all is well and by the way I've got you on video fingering a pile of cash and drugs."

I needn't have worried... a little after nine McClure was on the line.

"Morning Ash, sleep well?"

"Never better Jim," I said trying to sound light, unconcerned, "what's happening?"

"Couple of things I want to discuss, to do with that disc you gave me, but not on the phone. Can you come in—say a couple of hours?"

I promised to be there at eleven, and ended the call. As I put the phone down I realised my palms and upper lip were sweating—I'd never been so pleased to end a conversation, but I had to prepare for the next phase.

I cleared through the Met ground floor security shortly before eleven o'clock, and made my way to level five and McClure's office. I suddenly noticed Sergeant Shepherd sitting at his desk, off to my left. Damn it... I hadn't given him a thought through all this. I could only hope nobody had given him grief over our little sortie at the adult shop. Particularly McClure, given his involvement—and the sergeant knew nothing of that, yet! I should have alerted him.

Cindy was at her desk, looking magnificent! Given my hasty retreat a couple of days earlier, I was not sure how this would go.

"Hi babe," I said softly, smiling and holding out my hand, "sorry about the other evening. Maybe we can have another go at getting this right?"

Cindy lifted her head, smiled slightly in return and looked sideways at the boss's office. She put her finger to her lips. "Shhh . . . the inspector is waiting," she said rising and opening the door for me.

McClure, thankfully, was alone. As I entered he stood and walked around his desk to me. We shook hands . . . warmly . . . just like best buddies.

CHAPTER
SEVENTY-THREE

A sh, I don't want to beat about the bush. We have a situation developing here," McClure began matter-of-factly.

"Yes," I said tentatively, "a situation?"

"I'm just worried that you're going to be in the shit. It's partly my fault, as I've let you proceed under your own steam, and not given you the backup needed. I don't want you crucified in the process."

Crucified? Me? So I'm going to be in the shit? How in the hell could I be in the shit—McClure was the one on camera with his hand in the till? Unless he knew about the adult shop raid!

Enough of this crap . . . time for me to take the plunge. "No Jim, there's been no problem regarding backup, it's the volume of evidence which has come to light . . ."

McClure held up his hand to stop me. "I've had that evidence checked—not that I really needed to—because the person on camera handling those drugs—and you're right, *it is ice*—is Alvarez."

"Yes!" I bellowed, snapping a fist-pump, "I knew it—I *knew* it was him." But the evidence capturing McClure, that still required an answer, and I was the one who had to put it to him.

"Jim, there are *other* important questions which need to be answered," I said taking a deep breath, "particularly the pile of drugs and cash which Alvarez separated out. We have that on tape too . . ."

"I know, I know," cut in McClure again, "that was put there for a reason. A very specific reason, and I'm surprised, no relieved, you haven't mentioned it. Maybe, of course, you don't know about it?"

"Know about *what*?"

"Somewhere there will be a tape of *me* handling that supply. I haven't seen it, but the fact all this other stuff is recorded, means that will be, also. See Ash, I haven't been entirely straight with you."

Hell, I thought, here comes a full-blown confession and I haven't had to ask a single question about it. About time I got some direct answers, but I said nothing. I let him continue.

"We've been tracking Alvarez for years. Over time, we arrested a number of his underlings—the odd street dealer, a couple of guys who ran some warehouse storage for him, those sort of people—but of course he was the main prize. We made it harder for him to maintain his channels. Problem was the harder we made it for him, the more difficult he became to get to. He seemed to withdraw."

It occurred to me this line was not heading in the direction I had assumed. No confession at this point. The DCI continued.

"A couple of years ago we launched a covert operation, to get someone inside his inner network. But it had to be somebody senior—someone who could guarantee him something he didn't already have. Over a period of months we let it be known that a senior officer of the Met could be bought. That officer would guarantee his supply lines could operate uninterrupted, for a fee. That somebody—the senior officer—was me."

"Right," I said as this new information sank in, "so when you took that supply and cash from the manager's office, that was your fee... sanctioned by The Yard. *You* maintained his supply lines... called off the dogs?"

"Precisely," continued McClure, "we've let him operate unhindered for a couple of years, waiting to get evidence of him, directly, handling the shipments. He was never near it—always done by somebody else—until recently. So I suppose some of the earlier arrests we made had some effect. It meant Alvarez had to become more directly involved. That was what was caught on the footage you gave me, and that was just the evidence I was after. We just had to figure out where it was, and how to get our hands on it."

"Instead it came to me," I said, "and that was *not* what you expected?"

"No, it threw me a bit. I couldn't work out who would have given it to you. But then I got to thinking... I had the description of the two men who conducted the 'search' of the premises . . . it wasn't hard to figure out who *they* were. Put two and two together."

"So you've known since yesterday, yet you said nothing?"

"It was no big deal for me—I knew you were doing the right thing, and with Shep helping you'd be in safe hands. I just had to make sure you weren't going to blow my cover with Alvarez."

"And the go-slow," I asked, "all the info I suggested you look at, with no result. Why did you stop?"

"I had to slow *you* down a bit—like I said, we'd put too much into this to have the operation compromised. That's why I got you over here after the murders. I needed someone I could trust—who wouldn't stuff this up—but I couldn't tell you. I needed you to become a pain in his arse! That way, I could separate what you were doing from the Met operation. Deflect attention away from us. So, you have my official apology for leaving you hung out on your own. The good news is it's had a pay-off of sorts."

"What sort of payoff?" I asked cautiously.

"Alvarez has had enough of your interference. After Victorian Secrets he was livid.

Well, he doesn't actually *know* it was you, but he's taken a punt and as far as he's concerned, *you're it*! As I'm *'on his payroll'*, he asked me to get you to a meeting. Naturally, I said I can work it out."

McClure then passed me his card with a handwritten Mayfair address.

"This evening Ash, you and I are to meet with Ernesto Alvarez, undisputed king of the United Kingdom drug trade. Six o'clock at his residence—Park Lane."

CHAPTER SEVENTY-FOUR

I left McClure's meeting feeling decidedly troubled; edgy. So he wasn't on the take? Maybe! An official sting apparently; if it was true! That made me feel somewhat better, but I couldn't figure out why *he* had so readily agreed to my attending this meeting with Alvarez. Didn't *I* have a say? What did Alvarez want? Surely he must have demanded *something*! One thing was certain—I wasn't being invited for a cup of tea and friendly chat!

As I left the Met office I passed Cindy. An idea came to me at that instant, so I stopped by her desk. After all, she had handled herself so well in Toulon, *professionally speaking*, she might be useful this time.

"I've got an assignment tonight and thought you might like to come along—interested?" I asked, raising an eyebrow.

"Maybe," she smiled, "depends what, where and most importantly, *who with*." She gave me one of her sultry glances—the *hook*!

"Ahhh . . . top-secret, but I think you'll find it interesting." I wrote down the address from the card McClure had given me. "Outside here—a little before six?"

"See you then," she purred, resting her chin on her hands and gazing up at me, without checking at the address.

Damn it, Todd, I thought, leave before you *lose control*.

I moved toward the lifts and spotted Sergeant Shepherd still at his desk, beavering away. He momentarily looked up, and I cocked my fingers to my ear making a 'ring me' gesture. He nodded, and I let myself out of the building as quickly as possible.

I needed to make some plans; I had half a day before this meeting, and I had to be ready. Ready for what? I didn't know, but my belly said get organised for it anyway.

First, a reconnaissance of the address McClure had given me. Better know where in the hell I would be, nearby buildings, cross-streets, that sort of thing.

I found a cab, and headed for my hotel, via Park Lane.

CHAPTER
SEVENTY-FIVE

C harles was on duty at the concierge desk. I stopped and pulled him aside. "I need a sheet of heavy, hard plastic about a foot square and access to an angle grinder. Can you arrange it?"

He looked around somewhat nervously, then nodded. "I–I think so, about an hour?" I slipped him a twenty for the purchase and headed to my room.

First thing to do was pack. Everybody now knew where I was staying, and I had no intention of being an easy target for Alvarez, or anybody else. It kept niggling—this feeling somebody always seemed to know where I was, where I was heading. That, also, was something I intended to asked McClure—see if he had any intelligent ideas on it. Surely *he* wasn't feeding information out . . . as part of his supposed Alvarez double-cross?

I rang Qantas and luckily they had a seat on a flight leaving Heathrow later that evening—they *always* had a seat for an Australian Federal Policeman. Whatever might happen at this meeting, I had decided—*I was out of here*! Even better, a late check-in was okay—I thought I'd probably need it!

I called Sally. God knows this case had taken some strange directions, and I found it so easy to *forget* to keep in touch. The call went to message bank—maybe she was working late again—so I left her a quick "hi darling", saying I'd be home about seven the morning after next.

I thought again of ending with "I love you", but I baulked—it just seemed insincere, from both of us. I'd have to address *that* face-to-face. I also said that if I was not on QF2, she should call Sergeant Shepherd of the Metropolitan Police—as *soon* as possible.

There were a couple of quick knocks on my room door. I opened it and Charles hurried in carrying a rectangular package wrapped in brown paper. He said nothing, placed it on the table and quickly ripped off the wrapping. Inside was a piece of heavy clear plastic about eighteen inches by one foot. "Hope this is okay—it was all I could get at short notice."

It was perfect. We dropped down to the hotel basement workshop, where he set me up in a corner complete with workbench, vice and angle grinder as requested. "What do you need this for?" he asked nervously.

"Watch—I'll show you," I said taking a felt-tip marker and drawing a number of five pointed stars. "You've heard of ninjas—ancient Japanese warriors?"

Charles nodded.

"They were very clever with weapons. One of their most convenient was called a shuriken, or what we call a star knife. Normally they're made of stainless steel, but I haven't got much time . . . and I need something a metal detector can't pick up."

Charles watched quietly as I cut out four stars, carefully grinding the point and sides of each blade to a razor sharp edge. Finally, I drilled a hole through the middle of each.

"That should do," I muttered quietly, holding up each one to inspect it against the ceiling light. "A bit lighter than ideal, but you know what they say about beggars and choosers?" I said, winking at him.

"Oh, I forgot—your change," said Charles, digging various notes and coin from his pocket.

I waved him away. "Keep it, buy yourself a beer—you've earned it." And I meant it—he was smart, interested, and a good learner. Also, he didn't seem to mind taking a risk or doing shitty little jobs. With the right mentor, he could make a terrific detective.

"Charles," I said as we travelled back up in the lift, "I'll be checking out a little later—about five-thirty. Can you book me a taxi and look after my luggage? I'll have a Sergeant Shepherd from the Met collect it around six. Please make sure nobody else touches it. Oh, and thank you for all your help. By the way, I'll get the sergeant to call you tomorrow, but I think by *then* it should be safe for Ryan to come back to work."

We shook hands, and I made quickly for my room. Just as I entered the sergeant rang.

"Quick question," I asked, "are you aware of any undercover operation over the past couple of years on Alvarez—official or other-wise?"

"No sir—not heard a thing. Except for us of course."

"Never mind. Sergeant, tonight I have a meeting and I may need your assistance."

As usual, the sergeant was only too pleased to help. He would arrange a taxi and collect my luggage—three bags—from The Landmark at six-fifteen, then be standing by just off Park Lane for a trip to the airport.

I showered, changed, and checked my weaponry. I always carried two Glocks—new and old—and I much preferred the older. I packed the old one in its holster in my bag, and left the new for 'secreting about my person', as they say in the police files. I assumed it would be found upon my arrival at the meeting.

I tucked the star-knives into an inside pocket, and my plasticuffs into another.

Ready!

I noticed the time was nearing five-thirty. One last check of the room to make sure I had everything, then down to reception for check-out. Charles attended to everything smoothly and took my bags.

"I'll look after these sir—Sergeant Shepherd right?"

"Thanks again Charles," I said shaking his hand for the last time.

Then I stepped out onto the forecourt into my waiting taxi, and took a deep breath.

"Hello sir," said the driver, "Park Lane I believe? Magnificent, tranquil evening sir, isn't it?"

"Yes, thank you driver." I sure as hell hoped *he knew* something I didn't.

CHAPTER
SEVENTY-SIX

I arrived outside the address McClure had given me, about five minutes before six, where Cindy was waiting out front. A modern looking building; I couldn't make out whether it was an old building refurbished, or brand-new. Either way it had an impressive façade.

I paid the cab driver, walked over and kissed her lightly on the cheek. "What's the big secret operation," she asked, a quizzical look on her face.

"You recall our big-time drug lord—the one we suspect is behind all our killings?"

Cindy just stared up at me and nodded.

"Well, he wants to meet me. Your boss, McClure, has arranged it, and I thought you'd like to come along. Maybe you can watch my back," I laughed. "Let's go," I said taking hold of her hand.

I strode over to the security entrance and pressed the intercom for apartment fifteen zero one. A clipped English accent answered.

"Yes—your name please."

"Todd, Detective Commander, Australian Federal Police. I believe you are expecting me. Oh, and my assistant is with me also, but I imagine you can see that."

The voice instructed us to take the furthest left of three lifts in the foyer. I noticed the lift contained only three levels; parking, ground and fifteen. Ah, the trappings of success—a private express to the penthouse. We exited to a large, double-height, marble lined foyer, with a security camera set in a high right-hand corner.

A solid, swarthy-complexioned man in a suit came through a white-painted, double entrance doorway. I recognised him instantly ... the driver who featured so heavily in our recorded footages. I resisted the urge to comment.

"Would you mind raising your arms up and out please, sir—I need to check for weapons. We don't allow any, you understand." The very pukka accent seemed completely at odds with the physical presence.

"Of course, but let me save you the trouble," I said, reaching into my belt slowly, "I always carry this." I handed him my Glock, then spread my arms and legs anyway, inviting him to continue his search. He gave me a cursory inspection without touching.

"Thank you sir. That will be all."

Phase one complete; I breathed a quiet sigh of relief through pursed lips.

He then looked at Cindy, who was wearing a short, body-hugging skirt, a cream sleeveless blouse, and a short-waisted, red coat. Not much room for an arsenal in there! The doorman walked around her quickly, and barely cast her a glance.

"Please come in—Mr Alvarez is waiting."

CHAPTER
SEVENTY-SEVEN

The living room was huge—a vast area of white marble tiles and white painted walls, which were covered in enormous, vibrantly coloured works of art. There were two distinct seating areas, one comprising plush, oversize black sofas surrounding a large fireplace, the other a scattering of armchairs occupying a corner which led out to a long, tiled balcony.

The whole expanse was surrounded by floor-to-ceiling glass and, except for the view-space taken up by a neighbouring building, overlooked what seemed to me to be all of the city of London. It was bathed in a calm, yellow-grey hue created by the setting sun, which bounced off the tops of the buildings.

Seated at the end of one of the sofas, near the fireplace, was DCI McClure, now dressed casually in jeans and open neck shirt; obviously off-duty. Opposite him sat a balding grey-haired man, formally dressed in a dark blue suit and tie, and who I recognised immediately from the various security footages I'd seen.

Ernesto Alvarez!

Neither man rose. There was an awkward silence whilst I stood there looking at each, Cindy by my side, and they in turn taking in the sight before them. It was McClure who spoke first.

"Ash, let me introduce Mr Alvarez. Mr Alvarez, please meet Detective Commander Ashley Todd from the Australian Federal Police."

Alvarez nodded slightly and pointed to one of the sofas in the group.

"Please sit."

"Thank you, but I don't intend to stay long, so I'll stand," I said, without a hint of emotion. I didn't want to get too comfortable in his presence—after all, this man took no prisoners—and I wanted to keep my options open. "You wanted to see me?"

"I'll come straight to the point," said Alvarez abruptly. The accent was interesting; English but with a definite undercurrent of American, and even some residual Latin American from his childhood I guessed.

"I run a very big business here, and lately key people in my organisation have run into trouble, from *you*. I want *you* to disappear—to walk away, and stay away, and for that I'm prepared to pay. All we need to do, is determine your price."

I looked over at McClure, who said nothing but merely raised an eyebrow and shrugged a little. A "he's in charge, what can you do?" look. Clearly, he was going to be of no help.

I stared straight back at Alvarez.

"Mr Alvarez, I was brought here to help solve two murders—men who were known to me from many years ago. Since then, there have been murders of other people associated with the case. Whichever way *I* look, it all points back to one person—*you*! You are the common theme in their lives, or more precisely, the *end* of their lives!"

Alvarez remained seated, glaring at me, his face reddening. I was in pretty deep, so no turning back now. I quietly took a deep breath and continued.

"I don't need, or want, your money. As far as I can see, taking money from you leads to only one conclusion—*death*."

I shot another glance at McClure. He looked away, staring somewhere between his shoes and the large coffee table in front of him.

I resumed addressing Alvarez.

"I don't know if I have enough evidence to charge you with murder now, but conspiracy to murder? I think so. However, what I *do* have is all the evidence I need to arrest you for dealing in a prohibited drug. If I were you, I'd take a good look at all this—it maybe some time before you see it again, *if ever*."

"Ash, please, I don't think it's necessary . . ." McClure started.

Alvarez exploded with rage.

"You fucking Australian turd. Who do you think you are? You will *not* arrest *me* for anything!" He hauled himself to his feet; as he did so McClure also stood, and I was aware of somebody entering the room behind me. I turned my head slightly and caught a glimpse of the driver, who had disappeared through this conversation, and had now returned. Cindy also moved a couple of steps away.

Suddenly, I felt *very alone*.

"Mr Alvarez... Ernesto Alvarez," I said adopting my most formal policing tone, "I am arresting you..."

"Be *fucked* you are," Alvarez yelled waving his right arm in the air.

At that moment I heard a sound behind me. *My gut screamed danger*!

I turned and dropped to the floor just as a weapon discharged. The driver unleashed three quick rounds. I reached into my coat pocket as I landed, and in one rapid movement reefed out a star-knife and flipped it hard, straight at the driver. The razor-sharp point hit him mid-forehead, just above his nose and he dropped to the floor, air loudly expelling from him as he crashed.

I swiftly rolled across the floor two or three times, grabbed the pistol and jumped to my feet. I glanced quickly at Alvarez, then at McClure who was lying on his back next to the coffee table. I checked the driver's pulse. He wasn't dead; but stunned—maybe in shock. Blood was slowly seeping from his head wound.

I shoved the pistol into my belt, and looked at Alvarez.

"Maybe I should add the charge, *attempted murder of a policeman.*"

Alvarez stood, beetroot red, saying nothing.

I took a couple of steps towards the sofas and peered over. Blood was pouring from McClure's chest. The driver had missed me and *taken out the DCI.*

"Cindy," I said, not wanting to take my eyes off either Alvarez or his driver, "check out McClure can you? See if he has a pulse."

Cindy eyed Alvarez nervously, bending down beside McClure's prostrate body. She looked up at me, eyes wide.

"I–I think he's dead."

"You bastard—*you've* caused all this," screamed Alvarez at me.

He took a couple of quick steps around the end of the coffee table and turned towards the windows. I followed his movements like a hawk. He turned back to me screaming again, *"you've caused this."*

At that moment I caught a glint, a shimmer from the neighbouring building—like sunlight bouncing off metal. And something moved! I couldn't make it out clearly, but in a flash I realised—an Alvarez accomplice! *A sniper*?

Alvarez put his hand on top of his head, arm bent, then snapped it straight.

"*You* must be taught a lesson," he bellowed.

Cindy suddenly jumped up from McClure's side towards Alvarez and screamed.

"*Daddy, no! Enough!*"

In that instant, the glass of a huge picture window shattered, and Cindy dropped like a stone. I did the same.

My body felt numb but my mind was reeling. What the fuck had she said? Daddy! She called him *daddy*? How could that be—is *he* her *father*?

Then from Alvarez came a gut-wrenching cry.

"*Oh my God—no, no, no—my beautiful girl. What have I done to you*?"

I remained on the floor—there was no telling who else was lined up for this attack. Alvarez was on his knees, bent over Cindy's body which I still couldn't see. He stood up crying loudly, and sat on a sofa, shaking. He was now looking like coronary material.

"You got any more surprises out there," I asked, "or do I have to kill you to take you in?"

"No, no—it's okay," Alvarez mumbled quietly. The total change in his attitude was sudden, immediate. From sheer arrogance and rage, he now looked like a beaten man. He slowly stood up and walked, stooped, from the living room out onto the terrace.

I crawled around the end of the sofa. A massive blood pool had formed ... and there was my beautiful Cindy. *Dead*! She was lying face down, her head strangely twisted sideways, and eyes wide open ... staring vacantly. There was no doubt the bullet, which must have come from an M107, was meant for me. Cindy had taken the hit.

Never, in my wildest dreams, could I have imagined an end for us *like this*!

I longed to hold her again, to protect her somehow, but I still had this psychopath ... her *damned father* apparently ... and his driver to deal with. And *an assassin* out there somewhere!

Lying on the cold, tiled floor with blood staining the arm of my jacket, I stroked her face, gently closed her eyes, and kissed her goodbye.

CHAPTER SEVENTY-EIGHT

I crouched low behind the sofas, moved over to the driver, and cuffed him. I then moved along the far wall of the living room until I reached the circled group of armchairs. I picked a high-back one, which shielded me from the windows but allowed me to see along the terrace. Alvarez was standing, still shaking, gazing at nothing over London.

The whole scene was surreal. For a moment I felt totally removed from it . . . like observing from afar.

"Is Cindy *really* your daughter?" I asked.

"Yes," he said, but offered nothing more.

It suddenly dawned on me how *blind* I had been. No damn wonder people knew my movements. From day one, Cindy was a direct communication line from me to ... to anyone. To McClure ... that was expected. But to Alvarez? It *had* to be her! Maybe it was *both* of them! What a *bloody mess*! Alvarez knew my every movement, all the time.

"How many others on the payroll?" I asked, as Alvarez continued staring over the city. "People of influence—how many more have you got your hooks into?"

There was a long silence before he spoke again.

"It's the formula, Commander, the same formula I have used around the world for more than forty years. The others—it doesn't matter how many there are—because you, *damn you*, have broken it. Whatever I want, I buy. If I can't buy it, I take it. Except you ..." and his voice trailed off.

I looked across at the driver who was beginning to stir, pulled out my phone, and began searching the contacts.

"Well, are you ready to come?" I asked Alvarez without looking up.

There was no answer.

"Mr Alvarez?" I said, turning my head to face the terrace.

I couldn't believe it! There stood Alvarez on the low, brick terrace wall, still facing over the city, arms spread wide in a crucifixion pose.

I ran out to the terrace. *"Mr Alvarez*!" I snapped, trying to get his attention.

He turned his head slightly and looked at me.

"You . . ." he said quietly, as he stepped off into the empty space. I raced to the edge and peered over.

There, one hundred and fifty feet below on a concrete awning, lay the shattered, lifeless body of Ernesto Alvarez.

CHAPTER SEVENTY-NINE

I retreated to the living room, slumped into a nearby chair, and took a long, deep breath as I surveyed the carnage around me. I sat for some time ... don't know how long ... just staring at the bodies.

McClure and Cindy ... were they a team ... a perfect foil for The Yard's legitimate drug busting? Or was she a plant ... a brilliant placement by a cunning, ruthless operator?

How could they do this ... all of them? So many dead ... all dead ... and for what damn purpose? This is called *life*?

Not that it mattered now. Tears began to well ... then I got angry. Christ I was angry!

"*Aaaarrgh ...*" I bellowed, smashing my fist hard onto the coffee table. A large glass vase toppled, shattering across the floor between the bodies of Cindy and McClure.

The noise startled the driver, and I noticed he was now staring at me, wide-eyed with fear. I sat a little longer, ignoring him, until I regained my composure.

I had two calls to make.

I dialled Franch. It went to voicemail, so I left a message.

"Mate, I haven't got long but I want you to call Tommy. Tell him everything is even now . . . I've settled Joe's account in full . . . and Hell has a new member. I'll be in touch."

I scrolled my contacts for 'S' and pressed the call button. "Yes sir," answered the familiar voice of Sergeant Shepherd.

"You nearby?"

"Right outside sir, taxi waiting with luggage."

I rifled through the pockets of the driver, found a bunch of keys and let myself down in the security lift. I handed the keys to the sergeant, along with a fifty.

"Sergeant, I'm sorry to do this to you, but I've left you a hell of a mess up there. Level fifteen—this key will get you there," I said separating the security key out.

"The driver is alive, everyone else is *dead*. Alvarez went over the edge . . . he's out the back. Oh, and there was a sniper next door. He was meant to get me, and he's just watched his boss take the short-cut downstairs . . . he's probably evaporated by now. The money is for your cab home later."

"No problem sir, I'll attend to it," he said in his matter-of-fact way.

I reached into the back of the taxi.

"This bag," I said separating the smallest from my collection of three, "contains evidence. You have the gun with the prints—this is the rest. Security footage of all of them sufficient to convict. Not that any of it matters now—it's over."

He nodded a few times, slowly. "I understand sir."

I put my arm around his shoulder, and shook his hand firmly.

"Shep, thank God for you. I'll give you a call when I get back with a full statement—it's not good up there and you'll need it. Now, if you'll excuse me—I've got a plane to catch."

EPILOGUE

Qantas Flight Two from Heathrow landed at Sydney's Kingsford Smith terminal at seven-forty-three on a warm, sunny, and slightly humid, Saturday morning. I peered out the window as we approached the landing, gazing over the bright blue waters of Botany Bay before touching down on runway 34 left. It never felt so good to be home.

I cleared through customs and collected my bags from the carousel. This time, I didn't pull rank—no special clearance. I was just happy to be here, and I didn't care how long it took.

It had been nearly twenty-four hours since I left London—a whole day had passed, and I had not had to deal with anything to do with Alvarez, McClure, murder, or drug dealing. It felt like some sort of time-warp—some strange disconnect between then, and now.

And then there was Cindy. I couldn't, no matter how hard I tried, get my feelings for her, or about her, in any order. In the course of three short weeks, I had gone from mild interest, to curiosity, to lust, and for a fleeting moment, maybe even to love. Now she was dead and all I could feel was a mixture of grief and betrayal. I couldn't sort out which one was real, but what I did feel was overwhelmingly sad. I couldn't get the picture of that beautiful face, even in death, out of my mind.

I stepped from the terminal into the morning sunshine. I reached for my phone which was still switched off, and fired it up. Once I had signal, it bleeped with a message. It was Sally, and it suddenly occurred to me I'd had no response from her to my London message. Had she even got it?

The text lit up the screen... *"Ash—not feeling well. Can u get cab? c u soon. xoxo. S"*

Oh well, one more taxi ride wouldn't make much difference. Of more concern was the fact she always seemed to be ill. What was that all about? The cab slipped along the freeway, cut through the back of a slowly awakening King's Cross, and in twenty minutes I finally pushed the key into the lock of my front door.

I opened it and the salty breeze off the harbour hit me. I breathed it in deeply. It was still early, but the nor'easter was already making its presence felt. Sailboats were flitting about on the water below—the eighteen footers were my favourite—and it wouldn't be long before the harbour would be abuzz with weekend racing.

"You there honey?" I called out.

Sally came out of the bedroom, dressed in a light negligee. She looked fabulous! Waaay better than before I had left—or was it just my memory playing tricks? She came over to me slowly and put her arms around my neck. I bent down and we kissed passionately.

"I'm so sorry," she said, "for all the trouble." *She* was sorry; I thought *I* was the one who should be apologising, as my mind momentarily flipped back to Cindy.

"Don't be silly—you've been no trouble. I'm sorry we haven't been able to talk—I've always been on the move. But every time I've rung, you've been at work, or out, or very tired, or sick. What is *wrong*—are you okay?"

Sally smiled a gentle smile, and gazed out at the harbour. Then she looked back at me and softly stroked my face. "My darling Ash— sit down."

We sat side-by-side on the sofa, and she obviously saw the look of confusion on my face. "Honey, I couldn't tell you—I didn't want to tell you. I knew you would be busy, and it would not be the right time. It would only complicate your work, so I thought it best to wait until you returned."

"Tell me *what*?" I sounded a little impatient, fearing what might come next. Whatever it was, I probably deserved it. "What couldn't you tell me over the phone?"

"It's true, I have been sick—and tired— but I wanted you to hear it from me, face-to-face. Honey, *I'm pregnant*—you're going to be a daddy!"

I put my arms around her again. Words left me! I was *speechless*! In that moment, morning sun streaming in off a cool harbour breeze, she looked and felt more magical than any person, *ever*, in my life.

R OSS CROTHERS has spent much of his working life in the fields of commercial finance and international commodity broking. Characters and events from these years have inspired this book.
He and his wife live in rural Australia.